Forged By Dirt
&
Whiskey

ISBN 979-8-218-64574-8

LCCN 2025906029

Book Cover by Noureddine (Nour E)

First edition 2025

Authors Note

This story is based on true events. Names, places, and timelines have been adapted for narrative clarity, but the heart of it is all the experiences, the bonds, the struggles, and the triumphs—are drawn from real life. Thank you for reading.

Prologue

Kevin's heart pounded in his chest, louder than the low hum of his idling engine. Blue and red lights pulsed behind him in the rearview mirror, painting streaks across the dark windshield. He pulled over slowly, hands trembling as he shifted the truck into park.

This wasn't war. There were no enemy checkpoints, explosions in the distance, or armored convoys, but somehow, this moment felt just as dangerous.

The officer's footsteps became louder as the cop walked towards him on the cold asphalt. Kevin rolled down his window, trying to steady his breath. The stale scent of beer clung to his shirt—three drinks, maybe four. He'd lost count.

This wasn't supposed to happen.

He was supposed to be at an AA meeting tonight. He was supposed to be fixing his life, proving to his wife, and to himself, that he could get sober. But something inside of him cracked. One beer turned into many, and here he was—sitting in his truck with shame thick in his throat.

How did it come to this?

He'd done his part. Served his country. Pulled his weight as a machine gunner in Afghanistan and worked hard as a Navy Seabee. He wasn't a hero, but he had been dependable—someone his team could count on. He'd earned rank, built bonds that felt more like family, and tried to carry himself with purpose and honor.

But none of that mattered now.

The cop reached the window. Kevin forced a smile.

"License and registration," the cop said.

Kevin handed over his license, registration, and quietly slid in his Navy ID, hoping—maybe praying—it would help.

The cop glanced at the ID and raised an eyebrow. "You're in the Navy, huh?"

One wrong move, one whiff of his breath, and it was over—his career, his marriage, everything. Kevin stared straight ahead, heartbeat thudding in his ears.

"How did I get here, again?" He thought to himself.

Part One: Pre-Deployment

Kevin Murphy's childhood was the kind people looked back on with nostalgia. Not perfect, but close enough. He grew up on Elmwood Drive, in a suburb northwest of Chicago where every house had a driveway and a front yard, and most people left their doors unlocked during the day. It was the kind of neighborhood where kids played outside until the streetlights flickered on, where summers smelled like fresh-cut grass and backyard barbecues, and winters were filled with the scraping sound of shovels against pavement.

The Murphy house was a sturdy two-story with beige siding that needed a fresh coat of paint and a screen door that slammed no matter how gently you tried to close it. The garage was always cluttered with half-finished projects—his dad's old workbench covered in sawdust, a broken lawnmower that had been waiting for repairs since Kevin was in elementary school. His mom kept the inside neat, though, filling the walls with framed pictures of little league games, school portraits, and family vacations to Wisconsin Dells.

Kevin's parents weren't rich, but they worked hard. His dad, Jim, was an airline pilot—an old-school, blue-collar guy at heart who believed in early mornings, honest work, and finishing your plate at dinner. His mom, Lisa, worked part-time as a nurse but was mostly a stay-at-home mom, always keeping the house running and making sure Kevin and his sister Emily stayed on the right path.

Emily was the kind of little sister who kept Kevin on his toes. Sharp-witted and stubborn, she had a knack for calling him out when no one else would. Growing up, she was always tagging along, determined to prove she could keep up with her big brother—

whether it was racing bikes down their quiet street or arguing over the remote. But beneath the sibling rivalry was a bond that ran deep. She saw through his tough exterior, noticed the shifts in his mood, and was one of the few people who could make him laugh when he didn't feel like it.

His best friends, Danny and Mike, lived just a few blocks away. Their world stretched across backyards, side streets, and the small patch of woods behind Mike's house, which they had claimed as their own. When they were younger, those woods transformed into battlegrounds where they fought imaginary wars, sticks turning into rifles, fallen logs into trenches. They'd argue over who got to be the hero, rolling through the dirt, shouting orders, pretending they were part of something bigger than just three kids playing in the suburbs.

They idolized soldiers, not because they fully understood war, but because it seemed like the ultimate adventure. Kevin would watch old war movies with his dad—*Saving Private Ryan, Black Hawk Down, We Were Soldiers*—leaning forward in awe at the way those men carried themselves. Brave, disciplined, unshakable.

"Those guys are the real deal," his dad would say, sipping his beer. "Takes a different kind of man to do that job."

Kevin wanted to be that kind of man.

But as he got older, the world got bigger. The games in the woods faded, replaced by backyard football and late-night video game marathons in Danny's basement. By high school, they were more concerned with driving, dating, and sneaking beers from their parents' garages than pretending to be soldiers.

Kevin played football—not the star of the team, but decent enough to start. Friday night games under the lights, the sound of the marching band, the feeling of pulling off his helmet after a long drive—it was the kind of thing that made him feel like he belonged. But he never had the drive to take it further. He liked the sport, but he didn't love it. Didn't eat, breathe, and sleep it like some of the other guys did.

Outside of football, he coasted. He was smart enough to do well in school but not motivated enough to try. His grades were good enough to keep him eligible for sports, but not impressive. Teachers called him "capable but inconsistent." His parents called him lazy.

By the time senior year rolled around in 2006, the people around him started making plans. Danny had a scholarship lined up at Illinois State. Mike was heading to trade school to become a welder.

"What about you, man?" Mike asked one night, as they sat in the bed of his old Chevy, parked in an empty lot near the train tracks.

Kevin took a swig of his beer and shrugged. "Thinking about the Navy."

Danny smirked. "You've been saying that since middle school."

"Yeah, well… I mean it this time."

Mike laughed. "Sure you do."

Kevin wanted to argue, but deep down, he knew they were right. He *had* been saying it forever. But when graduation came and went, he didn't go to the recruiter's office. He took a job at a construction supply warehouse instead, telling himself it was just temporary. A way to make money while he figured things out.

Only, he never really did. Kevin still felt a pull toward the idea of real adventure. He'd watch documentaries about soldiers and play video games about war. Deep down, he knew he wanted to be part of something bigger.

His dad, however, had other plans.

"Join the trades, Kev," he'd say over dinner. "You're good with your hands. You could be an electrician, make real money. Get a union job, buy a house, settle down. Military's a waste unless you're an officer."

Kevin didn't argue. He never did. But deep down, he knew the truth—he didn't want to spend his life stuck in the same dead-end job, in the same small town, punching the clock and repeating the same routine day after day.

Still, knowing what he didn't want didn't help him figure out what he did want.

Kevin never meant to stay in town after high school.

For years, he had told himself he would enlist. It was his plan—the only plan he ever really had. But when graduation came and went, he found himself standing still while everyone else moved forward.

Danny left for Illinois State that summer, texting him every now and then about football games, college parties, and late-night drives to Taco Bell with people Kevin didn't know. Mike started his welding program and was already talking about the money he'd be making once he got certified. Meanwhile, Kevin was working at a construction supply warehouse, stacking pallets of drywall and loading trucks for contractors who barely looked at him.

The job was supposed to be temporary. A way to make some money while he figured things out. But weeks turned into months, and months turned into years. The pay wasn't terrible, but it wasn't great, either—enough to cover bar tabs and gas money, but not much else.

At first, it wasn't so bad. There was a certain ease to it—clock in, move stuff around, clock out. No homework, no tests, no expectations. After work, he and the other guys from the warehouse would head to O'Malley's, the local bar where half the town seemed to gather on any given night. They'd drink cheap beer, shoot pool, and bullshit about nothing.

But as time went on, something gnawed at him.

It wasn't just that the job was mindless. It was that every day felt exactly the same. He'd wake up, go to work, come home, crack open a beer, and watch TV until he fell asleep. Rinse and repeat. It was like being stuck in neutral while the rest of the world kept moving.

He thought about the Navy sometimes. Thought about walking into the recruiter's office and finally doing it. But the idea of leaving—of actually *going*—felt too big. Too final. The longer he put it off, the harder it became to imagine himself taking that first step.

So he kept drinking.

At first, it was just a few beers after work. Then a few turned into five, then six, then nights where he didn't even remember getting home. More than once, he woke up still in his work clothes, the TV blaring some late-night infomercial, an empty bottle tipped over on the coffee table.

His dad started noticing.

"You're gonna piss your life away if you're not careful," he said one day, watching Kevin crack open a beer before noon.

Kevin took a sip and shrugged. "Relax, old man. It's the weekend."

His dad shook his head. "You used to talk about doing something with your life. Now all you do is drink and make excuses."

That one stung, even though Kevin wouldn't admit it.

It wasn't like he was some out-of-control drunk. He still made it to work. He paid his bills. But deep down, he knew he was slipping. The things that used to excite him—sports, going out, even the idea of joining the military—felt further and further away.

Then, one morning, he showed up to work still half-drunk from the night before.

His boss, Ron, took one look at him and sighed.

"Go home, Murphy."

Kevin rubbed his face. "I'm good. Just tired."

Ron crossed his arms. "You stink like a goddamn brewery."

"I—"

"You're done. Pack your shit."

There was no big argument. No pleading. Just a quiet, sinking realization that he had finally hit a wall.

Kevin walked out of the warehouse, sat in his truck, and stared at the cracked windshield for a long time.

Something had to change.

Kevin had never felt more certain about something in his life.

The morning after he got fired, he woke up feeling like hell—his head pounding, his mouth dry, his stomach twisted in knots. He knew exactly how the day would go if he didn't do something different. He'd lie in bed for a few hours, maybe nurse a hangover with some greasy food, then tell himself he'd figure things out *tomorrow*.

But *tomorrow* had already come and gone too many times.

So instead of reaching for another beer or scrolling through job listings he had no intention of applying for, he pulled on a hoodie, grabbed his truck keys, and drove straight to the Navy recruiting office.

It wasn't a flashy place. Just a small office tucked between a nail salon and a payday loan store, the glass door covered in posters of aircraft carriers and sailors in dress blues. The American flag hung limply from a short pole by the entrance.

He hesitated for a second. Then he took a deep breath, pulled open the door, and stepped inside.

A young Petty Officer sitting behind a desk looked up from his computer. "Can I help you?"

Kevin nodded. "I want to enlist."

The guy smirked. "Yeah? You sure about that?"

For the first time in a long time, Kevin was.

A week later, Kevin was on his way to the Military Entrance Processing Station—MEPS—in Milwaukee, where he'd take the ASVAB, go through the medical exam, and, if all went well, officially enlist.

The drive up from the suburbs was quiet, just him and his recruiter. Chief Henderson had been in the Navy for over twenty years, and he talked like a guy who had seen it all. He barely glanced at Kevin as he drove, offering a few last-minute words of advice.

"Don't be nervous about the ASVAB," Henderson said. "It's not rocket science. Just don't overthink it. And for the love of God, tell the truth during the medical screening. You don't want to get sent home over something stupid."

Kevin nodded, gripping his knee to keep from bouncing it. He wasn't nervous—at least, that's what he told himself. But as they got closer, a weight settled in his chest. This was real now. Not just something he talked about, not just an idea. By the end of the day, his life would be set on a path he couldn't undo.

MEPS was a government building, plain and efficient. Inside, it was all business. The place smelled like cleaning supplies and burnt coffee, and the walls were lined with motivational posters—things like *Integrity First* and *Be All You Can Be.*

Kevin and a handful of other recruits were shuffled into a room with rows of computers to take the ASVAB test on. The ASVAB test consisted of long math, reading comprehension, mechanical knowledge, and electronics. Some questions were easy, some made his head hurt. He wasn't the best at school, but he focused as hard as he could, knowing this test would decide his options in the Navy.

When he finished, he sat back, rubbing his face. Now came the waiting.

An hour later, a Petty officer called his name. "Murphy."

Kevin stood.

The man looked at the clipboard, nodding. "You did all right. Scores are solid—nothing crazy, but enough to get you some good job choices."

Kevin exhaled slowly, only then realizing he'd been holding his breath. One step down.

Then came the medical exam.

A group of them were sent down a long, cold hallway and into a series of rooms where they were poked, prodded, and questioned about every aspect of their health. Blood work, urine tests, eye exams. Standing in their boxers while a doctor checked for hernias. The infamous "duck walk" in a room full of half-naked strangers, wobbling across the floor like idiots to prove their joints worked.

At one point, an older doctor with thick glasses squinted at Kevin's medical form.

"Says here you had a broken wrist when you were fourteen."

Kevin swallowed. "Yeah."

"Plates? Pins?"

"No, sir."

"Full range of motion?" The doctor rotated Kevin's wrist, watching closely.

"Yes, sir."

The doctor hummed, scribbled something on his clipboard, and moved on.

By the time it was all over, Kevin felt exhausted, like he had run a mental and physical gauntlet. But when they called his name again and told him he was medically cleared, relief flooded through him.

Next up, picking his job.

Kevin sat across from a job counselor, a grizzled Chief who looked like he had been in the Navy since the dawn of time. The Chief slid a sheet across the desk.

"Here's a list of jobs you qualify for. Take your pick."

Kevin scanned the list.

- Aviation mechanic
- Culinary specialist
- Hospital corpsman
- Intelligence specialist
- Boatswain's mate
- Electrician's mate
- Builder
- Utilitiesman

Some of them jumped out immediately. He knew he didn't want to cook or work in a hospital. He wasn't exactly the intelligence type, and aircraft didn't interest him much.

"What's this?" He pointed to *Builder* and *Utilitiesman*.

The Chief leaned back in his chair, nodding approvingly. "Seabee jobs. Construction Battalion. You won't be on a ship—you'll be out in the field, building bases, running heavy equipment, doing real work."

Kevin thought about it. Physical work. Something real. Something that would give him skills he could actually use. His dad had always told him to get into the trades, here's an opportunity to join the Navy and work in the trades, win, win right?

"What's the difference between Builder and Utilitiesman?" Kevin asked

"Utilitiesman (UT's) focus on utilities infrastructure such as A/C and plumbing where Builders (BU's) focus on structural construction, carpenters." The Chief responded.

"UT sounds good, I'll take it," Kevin said.

The Chief smirked. "Good choice. Welcome to the Seabees."

Kevin signed the paperwork, and just like that, his path was set.

One final step. The oath.

They lined up in a small, sterile room, an officer standing in front of them. Kevin raised his right hand, his voice steady as he repeated the words that made it official:

"I, Kevin Murphy, do solemnly swear to support and defend the Constitution of the United States against all enemies, foreign and domestic..."

By the time he walked out of MEPS, he wasn't just Kevin Murphy anymore.

He was a future U.S. Navy sailor.

Telling his parents was the hard part. Kevin sat at the kitchen table, tapping his fingers against the wood as his parents stared at him. He had rehearsed this conversation in his head a hundred times, but now that it was actually happening, his throat felt dry.

Kevin had expected his dad to be skeptical—he always was when it came to the military—but he thought his mom would at least be relieved that he was finally doing *something*. Instead, they both just stared at him.

"You *what?*" his mom asked, her voice sharp with disbelief.

"I enlisted," Kevin said, keeping his tone steady. "Navy."

His dad leaned back in his chair, crossing his arms. "And you didn't think to talk to us first?"

Kevin clenched his jaw. "I'm twenty-two. Didn't think I needed permission."

His mom exhaled sharply, rubbing her temples. "Kevin… this isn't like signing up for a gym membership. This is serious. You'll be—" She stopped herself, shaking her head. "Why now? Why all of a sudden?"

He could have told them about getting fired. About feeling like he was going nowhere. About all the nights he lay awake staring at the ceiling, knowing deep down that if he didn't do something soon, he'd wake up one day at forty, stuck in the same dead-end cycle.

But instead, he just said, "Because it's time."

His dad shook his head, muttering something under his breath. His mom wiped at her eyes, and for a second, he thought she might try to talk him out of it.

But then she sighed and said, "What's your job going to be?"

Kevin relaxed, just a little. They weren't happy about it—but at least they weren't outright telling him he was making a mistake.

"Seabee... Utilitiesman" Kevin said proudly.

"What the hell is a Seabee?!" She exclaimed.

His dad chimed in "Construction workers, they build in combat zones and help with humanitarian efforts."

"Is that so bad?" Kevin asked

"I don't know." his dad responded, "Your Uncle Paul was a Seabee during the Vietnam war, you should talk with him, see if this is a good idea."

Kevin didn't want to speak to anyone else about this decision, he didn't want anyone to talk him out of it. He knew if he didn't go through with this, he'd regret it. He needed to prove to everyone and even more so, to himself that he can do this, and it was the right choice for him.

Emily didn't hide how she felt when Kevin told her he was joining the Navy. She crossed her arms, eyes sharp with a mix of frustration and worry.

"So that's it? You're just leaving?" she asked, her voice edged with something she wouldn't call sadness—but it was close. She had always looked up to Kevin, even when she pretended not to, and the thought of him being gone, of not hearing his stupid jokes or arguing over nothing, felt like a bigger loss than she was ready for. But beneath her frustration, she knew he needed this. She saw it in the way he talked about getting out, about doing something bigger. So, she swallowed her protests, forced a smirk, and said,

"Just don't come back thinking you're too cool for us." It wasn't much, but it was her way of saying she'd miss him.

Two months.

That's how long Kevin had to kill before shipping out to Navy boot camp. It should have been an exciting time, a countdown to the start of his new life. Instead, it felt like limbo. He wasn't a civilian anymore, but he wasn't a sailor yet either. Just… stuck.

And worst of all, his parents still weren't on board.

His mom barely spoke about it, pretending as if ignoring it would make it go away. His dad, on the other hand, didn't even try to hide his disappointment. He'd been quiet at first, but as the weeks passed, the little comments started.

"So, you think the military's just gonna fix everything?"

"You ever stop to think about what you're actually getting into?"

"Joining because you lost a job—that's real smart, Kevin."

Kevin did his best to brush it off, but it stung. He wasn't expecting a celebration, but part of him had hoped that once they saw he was serious, they'd at least *try* to be supportive. Instead, every conversation about the Navy turned into an argument, so he stopped bringing it up.

Fine. If they wanted to doubt him, let them. He'd prove them wrong.

His friends weren't much better.

They didn't understand why he had done it. To them, nothing had been wrong with the life he was living. So what if he bounced between jobs? So what if he drank too much? They were all doing the same thing.

One night, during Christmas break when all his friends were home, they were at their usual bar when Danny leaned back, smirking. "So, what's boot camp gonna be like? They gonna shave your head and make you do push-ups all day?"

Kevin rolled his eyes. "Something like that."

Mike snorted. "Man, you're gonna hate it."

Kevin shrugged. "It's only eight weeks. Not a big deal."

Danny grinned. "Think you'll even make it through?"

Kevin tensed. "What's that supposed to mean?"

Danny held up his hands. "Relax. I'm just saying, we all know you don't exactly like people telling you what to do."

Kevin exhaled sharply, forcing a laugh. "Guess I'll have to figure it out."

Deep down, he knew Danny wasn't entirely wrong. He *did* have a problem with authority. But that was part of the reason he *needed* this.

He didn't want to be the same guy forever.

Still, as the beers kept flowing, it was easy to slip back into old habits. Drinking too much. Laughing at the same dumb jokes. Forgetting, for a little while, that he was supposed to be moving forward.

Until one night, he almost threw it all away.

It was supposed to be just a few drinks. Nothing crazy.

But a few drinks turned into shots. Shots turned into a bad idea.

Before Kevin knew it, he was in the passenger seat of Danny's car, music blaring, flying down a side street.

"Danny, slow the hell down," Kevin said, gripping the door.

Danny just laughed. "Relax, man, we're fine."

They weren't fine.

Red and blue lights flashed in the rearview mirror.

Kevin's stomach dropped.

Danny cursed, pulling over. The music cut off. The car was silent.

A cop walked up, shining his flashlight into the car. "License and registration."

Kevin sat perfectly still as Danny fumbled for his wallet. The officer's eyes scanned the car, pausing on Kevin.

"You been drinking tonight?"

Kevin's pulse pounded in his ears. He hadn't been driving, but if this turned into a mess, *he* could be the one paying for it.

Danny put on his best innocent voice. "Couple beers, officer."

The cop studied him for a long moment, then sighed. "Drive safe. And slow it down."

Danny let out a breath. "Yes, sir."

The second they pulled away, Kevin turned to Danny, his voice low and sharp. "Take me home. Now."

Danny scoffed. "Relax, man, we got lucky."

Kevin clenched his fists. "No. *I* got lucky."

That was the last night he went out with them.

After that, Kevin kept his head down.

He ran every morning, pushing himself harder each time. He studied his Navy knowledge. Anything to stay focused.

His parents barely acknowledged his training. His dad just shook his head whenever he saw Kevin heading out for a run, like it was all some ridiculous phase.

The night before he left, he sat on the back porch, staring up at the stars.

His mom finally broke the silence. "You sure about this?"

Kevin nodded. "Yeah."

She sighed, wrapping her arms around herself. "You know your dad's just… worried, right?"

Kevin swallowed. "Could've fooled me."

She gave him a sad smile. "He doesn't know how to say it. But he's scared."

Kevin didn't respond.

Because he was scared, too.

But he was doing it anyway.

Tomorrow, he was leaving. No more late nights with his friends. No more waking up in his childhood bed. No more wasting time.

And whether his parents accepted it or not, he was going.

Kevin had expected boot camp to be grueling — push-ups until his arms gave out, endless runs in combat boots, screaming instructors in his face at all hours. But after the first few days at Great Lakes, he found himself… bored.

Sure, there was some yelling. There were early mornings, endless inspections, and perfectly folded uniforms. But physically? It was underwhelming. Kevin had pushed himself harder in high school football practice.

He was ready to build and sweat — ready for the kind of hands-on work the Seabees were known for. But this? This felt like a never-ending series of lectures, inspections, and marching in circles. He wasn't going to be stationed on a ship, so half the training didn't even seem relevant.

"Why the hell do I need to know how to navigate a destroyer?" he muttered under his breath one day in class as the instructor droned on about shipboard damage control protocols.

The other guys in his division took meticulous notes, but Kevin just sat back, arms crossed, tuning it out. He figured once he got through this formality, he'd be off to A-school learning real skills — construction, welding, plumbing. That was what mattered to him.

Still, he went through the motions. He learned to march, stand watch, recite his general orders, and keep his bunk inspection ready. But his heart wasn't in it. The Navy knowledge portion? He barely skimmed the study guides.

His RDCs noticed. He wasn't the worst recruit in the division, but he certainly wasn't a standout. He didn't cause trouble — he just seemed detached.

"You'd better tighten it up before Battle Stations," one of them warned one night after Kevin missed a uniform detail on inspection. "It's not just about lifting things and swinging hammers."

Kevin nodded, but the warning didn't really sink in. Not yet.

The worst day of boot camp was when they did the gas chamber.

Kevin had heard about it—how recruits were forced into a room filled with tear gas, masks on at first, then ordered to take them off and recite their general orders. But hearing about it and actually doing it were two different things.

When the RDCs led them into the chamber, Kevin's heart pounded. His mask was on, and for a moment, he could breathe fine. Then the order came.

"Masks off!"

Kevin ripped his mask off, and instantly, his eyes burned. His throat closed up. Snot and tears poured from his face.

"RECITE YOUR GENERAL ORDERS!"

Kevin tried to speak, but his lungs felt like they were on fire. "GET OUT!"

He stumbled toward the exit, barely making it outside before dropping to his knees, gasping for air. Man did that suck he thought to himself.

Firefighting simulations, knot tying and team drills all passed without much fanfare. He got through them. But when it finally came time for Battle Stations, Kevin got hit with the reality he'd been ignoring.

Battle Stations was a grueling 12-hour overnight test — the final challenge before earning your Navy ball cap and being recognized as a sailor. It was designed to simulate real shipboard scenarios, from flooding control to fire response to emergency navigation.

And that's where Kevin realized he'd made a mistake.

The shipboard knowledge he had tuned out? Suddenly critical. Each scenario required quick thinking and teamwork, and Kevin struggled to keep up. He fumbled during a damage control simulation, couldn't remember key terminology during an emergency muster, and felt completely out of his depth when tasked with relaying information across compartments.

His teammates noticed. One of them, a kid named Dawson, pulled him aside during a quick break.

"Dude, you've got to lock in. You're dragging us."

Kevin felt the weight of those words. It wasn't just about passing anymore — his performance was affecting everyone around him. That hit harder than any RDC's yelling ever had.

Something clicked. He shook off the fog, refocused, and started paying attention to the details. He didn't want to be the guy holding the team back. He leaned into every task, pushing through exhaustion, studying the diagrams on the fly, and backing up his teammates whenever he could.

By the end of the night, Kevin was running on fumes — but he had made it through.

When the RDCs finally handed him the Navy ball cap, it felt different than he thought it would. Not just relief but a hard-earned lesson in humility.

He hadn't respected the process. He'd thought he was above it — but he wasn't. Even Seabees needed to understand the Navy as a whole. Even builders needed discipline.

As he stood with his division that morning, wearing his new cap and watching the sunrise, Kevin knew he had a long way to go. But for the first time, he wasn't trying to shortcut the journey.

He was ready to do the work — all of it

Wichita Falls TX, was nothing like Great Lakes. The heat hit like a wall the moment Kevin stepped off the bus. The air was thick, heavy, and smelled faintly of jet fuel. But more than anything, it was the freedom that made A School feel different.

No more RDCs screaming at sunrise. No more standing at attention in tight formation every time you crossed a hallway. Life in Texas felt like a breath of fresh air — or at least it did at first.

Kevin was slotted for UT A-School — Utilitiesman — one of the Seabee rates focused on plumbing systems, HVAC, water distribution, and fuel systems. Pipe fitting, troubleshooting, building things from scratch — it came naturally. He wasn't just getting by anymore — he was thriving.

The classroom part was straightforward. Blueprints, material specs, pipe codes — all things he'd seen before helping out on side jobs growing up. And when they moved into the practical labs, it felt even better. While some of the younger recruits fumbled with threaders and fittings, Kevin moved with confidence and precision.

"Did you do this stuff before the Navy?" one of his fellow students asked during a piping lab.

Kevin shrugged modestly. "Worked construction back home. Picked up a lot."

"Well, keep at it," the student nodded. "You've got a knack for this."

Kevin appreciated the compliment. For the first time in a long while, he felt like he belonged somewhere — like his past mistakes hadn't ruined everything. This was his lane. This was what he was supposed to be doing.

But that sense of ease — that feeling of belonging — came with a dark edge.

Phase One of A-School was structured, just like boot camp. There were liberty restrictions, mandatory accountability checks, and curfews. But once Kevin classed up to Phase Two, the leash loosened. More off-base liberty. Less supervision. More free time.

And that's when the old temptations started calling again.

It started simple — a six-pack after class with a few other Seabees. Nothing crazy. Just relaxing after a long day of pipe layout and water heater installation drills. But soon it turned into nights out at bars downtown. Then weekends were spent drinking instead of resting or studying. Kevin told himself he was just blowing off steam. Everyone else was doing it too.

But deep down, he knew better.

Some mornings, he showed up to muster with a pounding headache, hoping no one noticed the bags under his eyes or the slow drag in his step. His instructors didn't say anything — his hands-on work was still solid. But he could feel himself slipping, just a little.

He wasn't spiraling — not yet. But he could see the warning signs in the mirror: the way he stared at himself a little longer each morning, wondering if this was how it started again.

One night, after a few too many drinks at a local dive bar, Kevin found himself stumbling back to base alone. The street was quiet, the night humid and still, and in that moment of isolation, the buzz wore off just enough to let the guilt in.

What the hell was he doing?

He had made it out of a dead-end town. He had gotten through boot camp. He had found something he was actually good at. And now he was risking it all for what — another forgettable night and another hangover?

Still, the cycle continued for a few more weeks. He wasn't proud of it. But in his mind, he hadn't crossed any lines yet. He was still functioning. Still passing every practical test. Still hitting his marks.

But the truth was, he was slipping back into a version of himself he thought he'd left behind in Illinois.

And whether he admitted it or not, the clock was ticking.

Despite the late nights, hangovers, and more bar tabs than he cared to remember, Kevin finished A School with flying colors. He had a natural talent for the work — threading pipe, troubleshooting water systems, mapping layouts — it all clicked for him. What came hard to others felt like second nature to him. He didn't even have to try that hard. That was the problem.

When graduation came around, Kevin was pulled aside by one of the instructors.

"You know you finished number two in your class, right?"

Kevin blinked, surprised. "Seriously?"

The instructor nodded. "If you had tightened up just a little more — showed up a little sharper some mornings, nailed a few more written exams — you would've been top of the list. But still, good work. You've got a future in this rate, Utilitiesman."

Kevin smiled and nodded in appreciation, but the praise stung just a little. He knew exactly what had kept him from being number one. The missed study nights. The bar tabs. The mornings he barely got through muster with a clear head. He didn't say it out loud, but he knew it wasn't his work ethic that held him back — it was the bottle.

Still, number two was nothing to be ashamed of. He told himself he'd buckle down after A School — get serious, stay focused, and leave the partying behind him.

But the Navy had other plans.

Two weeks later, Kevin received his transfer orders: ECS — Expeditionary Combat Skills School — Gulfport, Mississippi.

It was the next stop for every Seabee before heading out to their first command. It wasn't just about trade skills anymore. ECS was about preparing for combat environments — rifle training, convoy ops, land navigation, IED awareness, tactical movement drills. It was gritty, physical, and intense.

Kevin was pumped. This was finally what he signed up for. Boots in the dirt. Sweat on his back. Real-deal Seabee training.

The first week at ECS lit a fire under him. The instructors didn't mess around, and the training days were long, hot, and physically demanding. Kevin straightened up fast. Monday through Friday, he was dialed in — sharp uniform, squared-away gear, solid performance in every training lane. The instructors took notice.

"Murphy, you've got good instincts out here," one of them said during a small unit tactics drill. "You might make a hell of a squad leader one day."

Kevin stood a little taller at that.

But when Friday night rolled around, all that focus melted away.

The weekends in Gulfport were wild — a rotating door of dive bars, house parties, and barracks booze-ups. Kevin went from five days of discipline to two days of chaos. He told himself he earned it. Everyone needed to blow off steam. It was just part of the culture. It was the Seabee way, "work hard play harder."

But his weekends started getting heavier — longer nights, harder liquor, waking up on Sundays with little memory of how he got back to base. He'd slap on a fresh uniform Monday morning and pull himself back together, but he could feel the cracks forming again.

He was caught in a cycle — professional squared away during the week, reckless and sloppy by the weekend. And no one was calling him out on it. Not yet.

He was doing better than he ever thought he would. But deep down, Kevin knew he wasn't operating at full potential — not even close.

After graduating from ECS, Kevin was granted a short period of leave before reporting to his first command. It was a welcome pause—a chance to catch his breath and spend a little time back home before stepping fully into Navy life.

Arriving at O'Hare, Kevin was hit with the cold bite of the Midwest weather — sharp, gray, and damp. It was a stark contrast from the Gulf Coast humidity he'd gotten used to in Mississippi. But beyond the weather, something else felt different. He couldn't quite put his finger on it at first. He was home, but not really.

His parents were waiting for him at baggage claim — his mom gave him a long hug, tighter than usual, like she'd been holding something in for months. His dad offered a handshake that turned into a half-hug, stiff and awkward. That was just how it was between them.

"You look... solid," his dad said, giving him a once-over. "Bulked up some."

Kevin chuckled. "They feed us pretty well, and I've been in the field a lot."

His mom smiled, but her eyes were heavy with something else — worry, maybe. Hesitation.

The ride home was quiet, filled with small talk about the weather, neighborhood gossip, and how the dog had gotten fatter since he left. But Kevin could feel the unspoken weight in the air — the elephant in the room still hadn't moved.

That night, over dinner, his mom finally said what had been simmering.

"I just still don't understand why you chose this path, Kevin. I'm not saying I'm not proud… it's just not what we imagined for you."

Kevin didn't get defensive — not this time. He'd heard it before. He just nodded and took a sip of his drink.

"I needed direction," he said. "The Navy gave me that. It's not glamorous, and it's not what you pictured, but it's what I needed."

His dad chimed in after a pause. "I respect that, son. I do. Just… this world's changing. Deployments, combat training, all that — it's dangerous. You don't think we worry?"

"I know," Kevin said. "But for once, I feel like I'm actually doing something right."

They didn't argue. They didn't have to. The divide between understanding and acceptance was still there, but they were at least trying to meet him halfway.

The next day, Kevin met up with some old friends at a bar downtown — the same place they'd used to hang out after high school, the same beat-up booths and cheap pitchers of beer.

At first, it was easy. Laughs, stories, a few drinks. But soon the conversations turned sharp around the edges.

"So you just build stuff in the desert or what?" one of them asked, half-joking.

Kevin forced a grin. "It's a little more involved than that."

"Man, I don't know how you deal with all that military crap. Orders, inspections, living in barracks... sounds like jail with a paycheck."

Kevin felt his jaw tighten. They meant well — sort of — but they didn't get it. Not even close.

"I'd rather be in a uniform building something that matters than sitting around here doing the same thing we've been doing since high school," Kevin said, firmer than he intended.

There was a moment of silence. Then someone raised a glass.

"To Kevin," one of them said. "Even if we don't get it, we're glad you're still the same old guy."

But Kevin wasn't the same. Not really.

Later that night, after most of the group had left, one of his closest friends — Josh — stayed behind and leaned in across the table.

"You seem better, man," he said. "Like, more grounded. Even when you're drinking, it's not the same chaos it used to be."

Kevin nodded, but didn't answer right away. Josh wasn't wrong — something inside him had shifted. But he was still figuring out what that meant.

As he looked out the window at the rain falling on the empty street, Kevin realized that home would never feel quite the same again. Not because it had changed — but because he had.

And deep down, he wasn't sure if that was something to mourn… or something to be proud of.

Kevin had barely settled back into a rhythm after his short trip home when his orders came in: Naval Mobile Construction Battalion 40 — NMCB 40, known in the Seabee world as "The Fighting Forty."

Location: Port Hueneme, California. But there was a catch.

The battalion wasn't in California. Not anymore.

They were already deployed — boots on ground in Afghanistan — and Kevin was being told to report, pack, and be ready to fly out in two weeks. Fourteen days to get his entire life in order, get fully checked in, and be combat-ready for the first time in his Navy career.

There was no welcome tour. No slow transition. No time to ease into battalion life.

"Welcome to the Fleet," the chief at personnel admin told him with a smirk as he handed Kevin a thick packet of forms. "Clock's ticking."

Kevin stood in the admin office at Port Hueneme with a thousand things on his mind. While most of his classmates from A School were heading to shore commands or staying stateside for additional training, he was being fast-tracked into a real-world deployment.

It was exciting — but it was also overwhelming.

Gear issue was first. He spent an entire day running from supply warehouses to armory checkouts. He was issued everything from flame-resistant uniforms and plate carriers to a full MOLLE loadout, a Kevlar helmet, goggles, gloves, knee pads, and cold-weather gear.

Every item was checked, cataloged, and triple-signed. Any mistake — any missing item — would delay him or put him in hot water once he joined the detachment downrange. The Seabees didn't mess around when it came to accountability.

On top of that, there was the mountain of admin paperwork: deployment checklists, medical clearance, dental records, legal documentation, wills, next of kin forms, travel vouchers, and pre-deployment briefings.

Then came the family readiness session — which was mostly awkward silence for Kevin. He didn't have a spouse or kids, and his family back in Chicago was still lukewarm about his Navy life. The session reminded him just how alone he was in this transition.

At night, he returned to his temporary barracks room, a basic space with whitewashed walls and the hum of fluorescent lights. He sat on his cot, staring at the duffel bag he hadn't even begun to pack yet.

He didn't feel fear — not exactly. But there was a restlessness in his gut, a sharp awareness that everything in his life had suddenly accelerated.

He wasn't a trainee anymore. No more instructors. No more phases. No more theory.

This was real.

The next two weeks passed in a blur. Uniform fittings, shots, briefings, paperwork, last-minute training modules. He moved through it all like a machine, checking boxes, signing lines, staying focused. But somewhere between the packing lists and the pre-deployment safety videos, the gravity of it all started to sink in.

He was heading to a combat zone.

No longer just a Seabee-in-training. He was now part of a battalion in theater — and they'd be counting on him to pull his weight from the moment his boots hit the dirt.

He made a few calls home in the final days before departure. His mom cried softly but told him she was proud, even if she still didn't fully understand. His dad simply said, "Stay sharp and come home."

On his last night before he left, with everything packed and squared away, Kevin felt a strange emptiness on his final night in California. There wasn't much left to do but wait for morning—and waiting had never been his strong suit. That kind of silence left space for thoughts he didn't want to entertain.

So when a few of the other Seabees from his deployment detachment mentioned hitting the town for one last hurrah, Kevin didn't hesitate.

There were nine of them in total, a ragtag mix of trades—builders, mechanics, electricians, UTs like Kevin—young, loud, half-jittery from nerves, and half trying to act tougher than they felt. They piled into two cars and drove out toward a strip of neon-lit bars on the edge of town.

Eventually, they landed at a strip club just off a forgotten highway exit. The place wasn't high-end by any means, but it had cold drinks, loud music, and a kind of reckless energy that made it feel like the right kind of send-off.

Laughter, cheap whiskey, and that hazy buzz of adrenaline filled the air as the guys threw bills on the stage and cracked jokes like they didn't have the weight of a combat zone hanging over them. It was juvenile, maybe even irresponsible—but in that moment, it felt like survival. A last taste of home before everything changed.

Kevin wasn't really interested in the scene — he watched his buddies toss bills on stage and holler like they were invincible, but his thoughts kept drifting elsewhere. Somewhere quieter. Somewhere more real.

That's when he noticed her.

Jessy.

She wasn't dancing, and she wasn't drinking. She was sitting by the entrance with a soda in hand, arms crossed casually over a hoodie with her ball cap pulled low. She was one of them — a Seabee — newly assigned to the same command, also awaiting deployment. One of the guys in their group had invited her out, needing a designated driver to keep them out of trouble.

She was quiet, observant, not trying to impress anyone. That's what caught Kevin's attention.

Later in the night, when things calmed down and most of the group had burned out their energy, Kevin found himself walking alongside her out to the car.

"You always end up being the responsible one?" he asked with a grin.

"Someone's gotta keep you guys from wrecking your lives," she replied, dryly but amused.

"Fair enough."

They talked a little more during the drive back to base — just small things. She mentioned she had just checked into 40 too and would be heading to Afghanistan in a couple weeks. Her orders had been slightly delayed due to some admin holdup, but she'd be joining the battalion shortly after Kevin arrived.

That struck a chord in him — maybe more than he expected. Back at the barracks drop-off, Kevin lingered by the car while the rest of the group disappeared into the night.

"Hey," he said, glancing into the passenger seat where her gear bag sat. "What're you reading these days?"

Jessy raised an eyebrow. "Uh… nothing exciting. I've got an old copy of The Old Man and the Sea in my bag. Picked it up at a thrift store before I came out here."

"Can I borrow it?" he asked, almost sheepishly.

She tilted her head. "You planning on reading Hemingway?"

"Honestly? Probably not. I just figured it'd give me a reason to find you again once you get there."

Jessy smiled — the first real one he'd seen from her that night. "That's a pretty decent excuse."

She handed him the dog-eared book. Kevin tucked it into his pack without looking at it again.

The next morning, before the sun had risen over Port Hueneme, Kevin boarded his flight — sea bag slung over one shoulder, helmet strapped to the other, and Hemingway tucked between layers of his gear. He was stepping into the unknown, unsure of what awaited him on the other side of the world.

But he had a feeling he'd be seeing Jessy again soon — and that, somehow, gave him something steady to hold onto.

Part Two: Deployment

The wheels touched down hard on the tarmac in Kuwait City, jolting Kevin awake from a restless, uncomfortable half-sleep. The cargo aircraft groaned as it rolled to a stop, its metal belly creaking under the desert heat.

Kuwait International Airport—is a sprawling hub of beige-toned terminals and polished marble floors, where the desert heat presses against the glass even before you step outside. Inside, the air is cool and dry, humming with the low murmur of travelers and the rhythmic announcements in both Arabic and English. Fluorescent lights bounce off clean tile, and signs in gold lettering point toward customs, baggage claim, and transit lounges. Soldiers in uniform mix with civilians, contractors, and diplomats, all funneling through the gates in a swirl of cultures and languages.

The second the doors cracked open, the air hit Kevin like a tsunami — dense, dry, and smothering. It wasn't just hot. It was a different kind of heat entirely, something Kevin had never felt before. The blast of wind off the street felt more like a blow dryer on high than a breeze. The thermometer outside read 125 degrees Fahrenheit.

His uniform clung to him, soaked almost instantly. Dust blew in swirling waves across the pavement. It was only mid-morning.

This wasn't Afghanistan yet. It was a staging point — a waystation for troops moving into theater. But to Kevin, it already felt like he'd stepped onto another planet.

As he stepped off the plane and grabbed his sea bag, a single thought punched its way to the front of his mind:

What the hell am I doing here?

It wasn't a loud thought. It wasn't panic. It was quieter — heavier — like a dull ache behind the eyes. For the first time since joining the Navy, Kevin genuinely wondered if he'd made a mistake. All the talk of serving, of making a change, of finding direction — it suddenly felt a lot less romantic in the middle of a scorching, featureless desert.

He and the others were shuffled into a holding area — a series of large, air-conditioned tents with rows of metal cots and plywood floors. There wasn't much to do except sweat, sleep, hydrate, and wait for a flight into Afghanistan.

That wait dragged into a full week.

Seven days of nothing. No training, no mission briefs, no movement — just waiting.

They weren't allowed to leave the staging area. Armed guards patrolled the perimeter, and the days blurred into a haze of bottled water, MREs, and silence broken only by the dull whine of aircraft overhead.

Kevin passed the time however he could — cleaning his gear, checking and rechecking his kit, watching dust storms rise over the horizon. He found the Hemingway book Jessy had given him buried in his pack and opened it out of sheer boredom one afternoon. He didn't expect to connect with it — but there was something oddly grounding in the story of a man battling nature alone.

Evenings were cooler, but the isolation remained. The camaraderie Kevin had started to build in California felt distant now. Everyone seemed preoccupied — some anxious, some withdrawn, some just killing time until it was their turn to board a flight deeper into the war zone.

He didn't talk much during those days. Mostly, he thought — about home, about his old friends, about the life he'd left behind in Chicago. About the bottle he'd leaned on for too long and the woman who'd handed him a beat-up book with a smile that lingered in his mind longer than he liked to admit.

He wondered if she was in the air already, on her way out here too.

Every day he checked the departure rosters obsessively. Names appeared, then disappeared. Flights were delayed, then canceled, then rescheduled again.

On the morning of day six, his name finally showed up on the manifest.

Flight to Kandahar Airfield — 0500.

It was time.

As Kevin pulled on his gear and cinched down the straps of his sea bag, he felt that same familiar tension tighten in his chest — a mix of nerves, anticipation, and something else he couldn't quite name yet.

The flight into Afghanistan left before sunrise, the inside of the transport aircraft rattling with gear, boots, and tension. Kevin tried to sleep but couldn't. Every bump in the air jolted him back to reality — this wasn't another cross-country hop. This was different.

When the back ramp finally dropped in Kandahar, Kevin braced himself for another wave of punishing desert heat — but it never came. Instead, a surprisingly cool breeze met him as he stepped out onto the tarmac. The air was still dry and gritty, but it carried a bite he hadn't expected.

"Thank God," he muttered under his breath as he adjusted his pack.

Kandahar Airfield was unlike anything he'd seen before — a strange mash-up of permanence and impermanence. Parts of the base looked like they'd been there for decades. There were CMU (concrete masonry unit) buildings stacked two and even three stories high — admin centers, communication nodes, hardened dorms for higher-ranking personnel.

But just as often, those sturdy structures were flanked by canvas tents, metal shipping containers, and plywood-framed structures with sandbags stacked high around them. Rows of porta-johns. Hesco barriers everywhere. Razor wire zig-zagged through alleys and entry points like it was trying to shape the chaos into order.

The base buzzed with movement — multinational troops, contractors, convoys moving in and out, aircraft humming constantly in the sky. Kevin watched helicopters sweep low overhead, their silhouettes ghosting through the dusk light, rotors beating like thunder in the distance.

His temporary barracks were inside one of the large transient tents — long rows of cots and gear stacked wall to wall. Nothing fancy, but it was quiet, and at this point, that was enough.

Still, the surrealness of it all hadn't faded. Kevin wasn't scared — not yet — but he was alert, overstimulated, aware that he'd just crossed a threshold. The galley was a huge tent structure surrounded by gravel walkways and heavy security fencing. Inside, the food was surprisingly decent — trays of hot chow, cold drinks, and oddly enough, fresh fruit.

Kevin stared at the bananas and oranges like they were artifacts from a better world.

"Fresh fruit," he muttered with a crooked smile. "What the hell."

He grabbed a banana, sat with a few other new arrivals, and tried to settle into the rhythm of the place. Everyone had that same look — half-wired, half-dead-eyed from transit. It was clear no one stayed at Kandahar long. It was just a pit stop — another waystation in the journey deeper into the heart of the deployment.

And that meant more waiting.

Kevin spent another four days at Kandahar, stuck in the same holding pattern he'd endured in Kuwait. This time, though, the air was cooler, the food better, and the infrastructure sturdier — but the anticipation gnawed at him all the same.

He checked the flight rosters daily, waiting for the one that would carry him north to Mazar-i-Sharif — the final leg of his journey, where his battalion, NMCB 40, was already dug in and operating.

He was ready to join them.

The flight into Mazar-i-Sharif was uneventful, just another leg in the long journey. But the moment the aircraft touched down and the ramp lowered, Kevin's stomach flipped. It was the feeling of landing in a foreign world — a place he'd only seen on television or in training videos, but never in real life.

The air in Mazar-i-Sharif felt different than in Kuwait or Kandahar, like it was carrying dust more than oxygen. The troops referred to this as moon dust. The landscape outside the airfield was barren, a patchwork of brown earth, concrete, and dilapidated buildings — the remnants of a country struggling against itself for decades. From the airfield, Kevin and his team had to convoy across town to Deh Dahdi, where their battalion was stationed. The convoy ride was nerve-wracking—his eyes scanned every rooftop, every alley, knowing danger could be anywhere.

The convoy that awaited him was typical for military operations here: armored trucks, and a variety of military vehicles. Kevin climbed into the back of an MRAP (Mine Resistant Ambush Protected vehicle); his sea bag slung tightly beside him. He was directed to sit in the seat closest to the gunner who was standing on a platform with his head and shoulders out the top of the truck at the same time operating a 240 Bravo machine gun. Multiple green boxes of ammo were laid at the gunner's feet. Kevin was instructed to hand up extra ammo box's if the gunner were to need some. The doors clanged shut with a deafening thud, sealing him inside the armored vehicle. His heart raced slightly; this was real now. He wasn't just in a holding area anymore.

As the convoy began to roll out, Kevin looked out through the narrow, reinforced windows and saw Afghanistan for the first time — not the sanitized, controlled environment of the base, but the raw, rugged reality of the country.

The roads were narrow and choked with dust. People lined the streets, walking in the heat, dressed in what Kevin could only describe as rags. Men wore loose tunics, women covered head-to-toe in black, their faces obscured, moving silently through the dust. Children played in the street barefoot, kicking around balls made from scraps of trash, while older men sat in small groups beside shops made of scrap wood and stone.

Houses dotted the side of the road, but they weren't like the homes Kevin had known. Many of them had only three walls, with the fourth open to the elements. Piles of bricks and rocks were strewn across the road, as if the buildings were still being constructed — or worse, never finished. The whole scene was a chaotic blend of poverty, survival, and resilience.

It struck Kevin hard. He'd seen poverty before — in his hometown, in other parts of the world — but this was different. This was a country torn apart by decades of conflict, a place where the concept of "normal" had long been replaced by survival.

As the convoy rattled through the town, the difference between the way the people lived and the way Kevin had lived — and still lived — felt so glaring, so sharp. He thought about his old life back in the States, the days of worrying about his next paycheck, or if the local bar would have the game on that night. In that moment, it all felt trivial. Stupid. Pointless.

Never complain about anything again, he thought to himself, staring out at the people who barely seemed to have anything.

He couldn't help but feel a wave of gratitude for the life he'd had. His family, his friends, the opportunities he'd taken for granted. He had always known he was lucky to be American — but now, looking at the dirt roads, the makeshift shelters, and the people who had nothing, the realization hit him with a weight he couldn't shake.

He had been so caught up in his own struggles back home. Now, for the first time, he saw how small those problems really were in the grand scheme of things.

I'm lucky to be here, Kevin thought, his mind racing as the convoy continued on its path. **Lucky to be alive. Lucky to have had a chance to change.**

The convoy snaked through the streets, bumping over potholes and rough terrain. The sounds of the armored vehicles were deafening, but they were oddly comforting, like a reminder that he was shielded for now — that this was the part of the job that kept him safe. It felt real now, the weight of the place settled deeper in his bones.

As the convoy made its way out of the town, the last buildings gave way to wide, open fields. Kevin's mind wandered as the vehicle rolled over the uneven roads.

When they finally reached their forward operating base, Deh Dahdi II, NMCB 40's compound, Kevin's nerves were shot, but he was ready. This was his home now — his base of operations. The dust, the sweat, and the heat weren't going anywhere. He wouldn't forget what he'd seen in Mazar-i-Sharif, but he had a job to do now.

The convoy came to a grinding halt just inside the perimeter of Deh Dahdi II, forward operating base. The heavy sense of movement settled into a pause. Kevin dismounted from the MRAP, his legs stiff from the ride, his boots crunching against the gravel as he looked around.

The base was a maze of Hesco barriers, tents, and prefabricated buildings. It wasn't exactly what you'd call comfortable, but compared to what he'd seen out the windows of the armored truck, it felt like a palace.

Before Kevin had time to get his bearings, a pair of men approached him. One wore sunglasses even in the dimming afternoon light, the other held a clipboard thick with personnel rosters.

"You Murphy?" the clipboard guy asked, barely glancing up.

"Yeah, that's me," Kevin said, straightening his posture instinctively.

"Good. Welcome to 40" the other one said, finally peeling off his sunglasses to meet Kevin's eyes. "I'm Chief Carter. You're assigned to Bravo Company, ECP team."

Kevin nodded, unsure if this was good or bad news. He hadn't even had time to ask questions yet.

"ECP?" he repeated.

"Entry Control Point," Carter said, turning on his heel as if expecting Kevin to follow. "You'll be on gate duty— screening local national workers coming onto base and vehicle inspections."

Kevin followed, trying to process the rapid-fire information.

"It's not glamorous, but it's important," Carter continued. "You're the first line between the inside and outside. You see anything sketchy — you sound the alarm. You get complacent, someone gets hurt. Simple as that."

Kevin nodded again. It sounded straightforward, but nothing felt simple in this environment.

They reached a makeshift admin building — plywood walls, a window unit A/C buzzing in overdrive, and rows of desks piled high with radios, maps, and duty rosters. Carter introduced him to a few of the other Seabees most of them looked road-worn, sun-tanned, and indifferent to the new guy. A few offered a quick handshake or a half-smile. Most didn't say much at all.

"Your team will walk you through your duties tomorrow," Carter added. "You'll get a brief from the ECP LPO, and we'll get you on the rotation. Should have your weapon and gear issued tonight."

Kevin nodded. "Roger that."

Before leaving, Carter handed him a laminated post layout, checkpoint procedures, and the base's emergency action plan protocols. Kevin took it all in silently, his mind already shifting into operational mode.

"Any questions?" Carter asked.

"No, Chief." Said Kevin

Kevin followed one of the junior petty officers toward the barracks area, a long row of tents half-buried in sandbags. They were halfway to Kevin's tent when they ran into his new ECP team just coming off work for the day. "New guy!" a voice called out, drawing Kevin's attention. Walking in their direction were two people in dusty uniforms: BU1 Hill, the Entry Control Point LPO (Lead Petty Officer), and BU2 Blair, his assistant. Hill was stocky and strait-laced, with a commanding presence but a welcoming tone. Blair, younger and a little more laid back, kept a sharp eye but greeted Kevin with a nod and a firm handshake.

"You're our new guy," Hill said, glancing down at the clipboard in his hand. "Welcome to Deh Dahdi."

Kevin nodded, trying to stay composed. "Happy to be here, Petty Officer."

"You won't be saying that after a few days," Blair said with a chuckle. "But you'll earn your place fast enough."

Kevin was walked over to his tent — his new home for the next six months — where he met his ECP teammates.

First was Brad, a stocky, barrel-chested kid who looked like he could bench press a truck. He had a loud voice, a permanent smirk, and a habit of bragging about everything.

Then came Sean, a wiry guy with a boyish face and an endless energy supply. He cracked jokes constantly and laughed at all of them — even the ones that didn't land.

"You'll like it here," Sean said, elbowing Kevin. "It's like summer camp, only with sand, weapons, and the occasional mortar round."

Kevin chuckled politely.

"What? That was funny," Sean said, laughing even harder. "Wait, wait — let me try again."

Finally, Ray appeared from his bunk, towering and quiet, with a thick red mustache that made him look like he belonged on a vintage recruitment poster. He gave Kevin a simple nod, then went back to organizing his gear without a word.

"He doesn't say much," Sean whispered, "but he's got the best sense of humor once you get him going."

Ray looked up and, without changing expression, muttered, "Only when Sean shuts up."

The whole tent erupted in laughter — even Kevin.

That first night, they sat around in their tent, talking about home and deployment, about gear, about the job. Kevin felt out of place at first, the new guy surrounded by an already-formed crew. But the ice was melting quicker than he expected.

BU1 Hill and BU2 Blair ran the ECP team with a blend of professionalism and realism. The next morning, Kevin met them on post. Hill gave him a quick rundown of the entry search protocol. It was straightforward, but exhausting: search every delivery truck that came through, search the drivers physically, inspect cargo — gravel, mostly — and ensure nothing slipped through.

"We've got dozens of gravel trucks coming in daily," Blair said, handing Kevin a checklist. "And guess what, boot — you're on driver search duty."

Kevin took the laminated sheet without complaint.

"Worst job," Ray whispered behind him, trying not to laugh.

Blair grinned. "Don't worry, new guy. After a week of sniffing diesel fumes and grabbing sweaty armpits, you'll be a pro."

Kevin cracked a smile but nodded. "Roger that."

He was led to the inspection zone — a small concrete pad lined with traffic cones and sandbags, set just outside the ECP gate. His job was to search the drivers delivering gravel — part of NMCB 40's mission, to expand the camp.

The drivers were local nationals, and though they were cleared through security screenings, Kevin still had to follow protocol: pat-downs, gear checks, visual inspection of the cab, undercarriage sweeps — the whole nine yards.

The drivers didn't speak English, so communication was a mix of hand signals and a few phrases he learned over time:

"Raise your arms."
"Sit Down."
"Face that way."
"Empty your pockets."

It was hot, dusty, and repetitive. Some drivers smelled like they hadn't bathed in days. Others looked terrified. He kept his tone calm, did his job methodically, and tried not to let the monotony get to him.

By midday, his uniform was soaked in sweat. His gloves were gritty, his face sunburnt under the weight of his Kevlar helmet. But he didn't complain. This was his job. He was new, but he was already earning respect.

Evenings in the tent were where the real bonding happened. After shifts at the ECP, soaked in sweat and dust, the team would peel off their boots, collapse onto their cots, and let loose in a way only those stuck in a warzone or prison together could.

The jokes came quickly — and they weren't PG.

"Jesus," Brad said one night, scratching his chest through his skivvy shirt, "I haven't seen a good-looking civilian woman in two months, and I'm about ready to propose to that girl on the poster."

"Just don't let her see your gut first," Sean chimed in, tossing a crumpled up sock at him. "She'll file for divorce before you can get home."

"Better than that toothless goat you were eyeing by the wire the other day," Brad fired back, grinning.

"Hey, don't kink shame," Sean replied with a straight face, then burst into laughter before anyone else could react. "C'mon, that was gold!"

Kevin laughed harder than he expected — not just at the joke, but at how ridiculous this whole place had become in such a short time. Somehow, talking about goats and fictional women made things feel normal.

Ray, sitting quietly near the back of the tent, was the only one not cracking up. He was sharpening his punch knife, eyes steady.

"You two keep talking, I'm gonna cut my ears off," he muttered.

Brad snorted. "Ray, you say that every night."

"Because every night you get dumber."

Kevin quickly learned that this vulgar, unfiltered banter was how the team communicated — it was equal parts humor and hazing, but there was no malice behind it. It was just the language of the tent. You took your licks, gave some back, and laughed until your sides hurt.

And if you didn't have a thick skin, you grew one quick.

When they weren't ragging on each other, they talked about everything from home to their worst hookups to who could go the longest without showering — not a small bet, considering how busted the plumbing was some days.

Kevin didn't need a warm welcome — he got that in sarcasm and fart jokes, in midnight wrestling matches over missing socks, and in Brad's snoring that could rattle a truck.

By the end of his first month, Kevin wasn't just the new guy anymore. He was part of the team. He knew Brad's lies from his truths, could predict Sean's dumb jokes before he even opened his mouth, and had finally gotten a nod of approval from Ray — which, as everyone told him, was the highest compliment you could get.

They were crude, loud, rough, and rowdy.

But they were brothers.

And Kevin, for the first time in a long time, felt like he belonged to something real. They even wore a Jolly Roger patch on their kit — a little outlaw symbol of their bond — and when Kevin received his own, it didn't just mark him as part of the crew. It made him feel like he'd finally found his place.

But for Kevin, something else was changing too — something quieter.

For the first time in a long time, he was waking up every morning without a hangover. No headaches. No sour stomach. No half-remembered nights filled with bad choices and worse judgment.

He felt… clear.

It was strange at first — this sense of balance and sharpness. He had gotten so used to dragging himself through the day back home, dulled by booze and regret. But now, out here, despite the dirt, the dust, the exhaustion — he felt good. Alive. Capable.

Even as he stood for hours at the ECP, searching gravel truck drivers, he realized he wasn't moving through the day half-numb anymore. He had energy. Focus. Discipline. He wasn't chasing a buzz or running from his own reflection. He was just doing the job — and doing it well.

He didn't talk about it. Didn't mention it to the guys. But deep down, he knew it mattered.

All it really was, was the absence of temptation.

Kevin wasn't complaining. He was feeling stronger every day — mentally, physically, and for the first time in years, emotionally.

He hadn't made it all the way out of the hole he'd dug himself into back home. But he wasn't sinking anymore.

He was climbing.

And even if the jokes were crude and the days were hard, he was part of something now — something that gave him purpose, pride, and maybe even a second chance.

One evening, as the sun dipped behind the distant mountains and the air finally started to cool, the tent filled with the familiar hum of idle chatter. Brad leaned back on his cot, hands behind his head, grinning like he'd already had his first cold beer in hand. "Man, first thing I'm doin' when we get back? Hittin' the bar—loud music, whiskey shots, and women who ain't wearing flak jackets." Sean perked up immediately, nodding. "I just want to hear a girl laugh without sand in my boots. I swear, even if she's a six, I'm falling in love." Brad laughed. "You always fall in love, bro. You'll be proposing before dessert." Even Ray cracked a smirk from his corner. "I'll just be glad to see someone who doesn't smell like foot powder and diesel fuel." Kevin chuckled, soaking in the moment. The thought of clinking glasses again, feeling the bass of music in his chest instead of mortar rounds, and being surrounded by some-thing other than camo and concrete—it sounded like heaven. The idea of freedom, of normalcy, felt almost surreal… but it was the kind of dream that kept them pushing through.

One night, the galley was buzzing with its usual noise—boots shuffling across plywood floors, silverware clanking on trays, and the hum of a thousand conversations echoing beneath the canvas roof. Kevin stood in line with his tray, half-awake and scanning the room absently, when he spotted her—Jessy. She was wearing a hairnet, a pair of food-safe gloves, and a tired expression as she ladled out mashed potatoes behind the steam line. But even under the fluorescent lighting, she still stood out. His heart jumped a little. She caught his eye and offered a small smile, recognizing him instantly.

As he stepped forward to collect his tray, Kevin leaned in slightly. "Didn't expect to see you slinging potatoes."

Jessy smirked. "Still got that same nice smile. I guess you made it out alright."

Kevin chuckled. "You getting off soon?"

"In about ten minutes. Why?"

"Come eat with me and my team," he said casually. "We're all degenerates, but you'll be entertained."

She paused for a second, then gave a small shrug. "Why not? Beats eating alone in the break tent."

Ten minutes later, Jessy joined Kevin at his table, sliding her tray down next to his as Brad and Sean immediately zeroed in like sharks smelling blood in the water.

"Oooohh, look who's got a dinner date," Brad said with a grin, elbowing Kevin. "Kev, you dog. Didn't know you had game."

Sean leaned in dramatically across the table. "Are you sure you're with the right guy, Jessy? I mean, he hasn't showered in three days."

"Four," Brad corrected, snorting.

Jessy laughed, rolling her eyes. "I've worked in this galley all week. Trust me, he still smells better than most of you."

That earned a round of laughter, and Kevin couldn't help but smile. The teasing continued through dinner—jokes about love at first sight, wedding invitations, and Kevin being whipped already. But underneath the laughter, something subtle passed between him and Jessy. A look, a smile, a moment of quiet understanding in the middle of the noise. For the first time since arriving in Afghanistan, the food didn't taste like cardboard and the tent didn't feel quite so far from home.

Over the next few weeks, a comfortable rhythm developed between Kevin and Jessy. They crossed paths often—sometimes in the galley, other times in passing around the camp. Jessy had a sharp wit that matched Kevin's dry humor, and their conversations, though brief, always carried a kind of ease that made the chaos of deployment feel a little more tolerable. They'd trade sarcastic quips, share stories about home, and occasionally sit together during meals when schedules aligned. The friendship felt natural, unforced—like something steady in a world that was anything but.

But as much as Kevin enjoyed her company, he kept a quiet distance. The thought of pursuing something deeper gnawed at the edges of his mind, but every time it crept closer, he pushed it back. It didn't feel right—at least not here, not now. Afghanistan was a place of constant tension, long hours, and mission-first mentalities. Between guard shifts, gear maintenance, and the weight of responsibility he carried for his team, Kevin couldn't shake the feeling that starting something romantic would be unfair—to her, to his guys, and even to himself. He respected Jessy too much to treat what could be something meaningful as just another distraction in a combat zone.

Besides, this place wasn't built for real relationships. Not with bomb blasts echoing in the distance and dust in your lungs. Kevin wanted to give her his full attention, his real self—not just the version of him that existed between patrols and chow lines. So, he stayed grounded in the friendship, content with the laughs, the shared moments, and the unspoken understanding that maybe—just maybe—there'd be a better time, a better place, when everything didn't feel like it was being borrowed from a ticking clock.

It was just after first light when Kevin got word—he and Ray were being reassigned temporarily to a convoy mission headed northwest to Sheberghan. The assignment was direct: build a helicopter landing zone for medevac operations to support the Sweden Special Forces operating in the region. Word was, the Swede's had been taking heavy casualties during raids and firefights in remote villages. Without a proper landing zone nearby, wounded troops weren't getting to advanced care in time. The goal was to cut down that critical "golden hour" — the time between injury and surgery — and save lives.

Kevin packed his gear in silence that morning, the weight of the mission heavier than usual. This wasn't just a supply run or routine patrol — this one had stakes that could mean life or death for people on the ground. As he double-checked his plate carrier, he glanced over at Ray, already strapping his gear on, eyes focused but calm as ever.

"Guess it's you and me again," Kevin said, tightening the strap on his helmet.

Ray gave a short nod. "Like a bad sequel."

Outside the staging area, they met the rest of their temporary team. Joe, the driver, was already doing checks on their MRAP — a tall, lean guy with grease-stained hands and chewing tobacco bulging from his lip. He barely looked up as Kevin and Ray approached.

"Better bring your neck pillows," Joe muttered. "Twelve hours of bumpin' and rattlin'. You'll feel it in your spine for a week."

Next came Dave, their fire team leader — late-20s, squared away, sharp-eyed, and no-nonsense. He wore his experience like armor. Kevin could tell instantly he was the kind of guy who'd seen a lot, probably more than he ever talked about. He offered a firm handshake and a short introduction. "I keep us moving. You keep your eyes sharp, and we'll all come back the same number of pieces we left in."

Lastly was Ben, the comms guy — younger, fresh-faced, and always carrying more gear than seemed physically possible. He had antennas sprouting from his ruck like a porcupine and never stopped adjusting something on his radio pack. "If it beeps, chirps, or breaks, I'm your guy," he said, offering Kevin a lopsided grin.

Together, the five of them stood around the armored vehicle, running last-minute checks as the sun fell lower into the sky. There was a tension in the air — the kind that came before every convoy, no matter how many you'd been on. The kind that made you double-check your mags, count your tourniquets twice, and say quiet prayers you'd never admit to anyone else.

Just before step-off, the convoy team was gathered under a battered canvas awning near the motor pool, the sun gone but only the stars shining. Everyone stood in a loose semicircle around the lead chief, a grizzled veteran with a deep voice that cut through the air like gravel against steel.

"This isn't a milk run," the chief started, eyes scanning the group. "You've got twelve hours of open road through some of the roughest terrain in the region. Intel reports possible IED activity along Route Bronze and the outskirts of Balkh province. Keep your sectors tight, don't get complacent, and follow convoy protocol like your lives depend on it—because they do."

He broke down the route—checkpoints, emergency rally points, comm frequencies, and rules of engagement. Everyone took notes, nodded along, some just stared blankly, knowing that briefings only prepared you for so much. The rest came down to luck, timing, and instincts honed by repetition.

As the chief wrapped up, the Chaplain stepped forward from the shadows, his uniform dusty and sleeves rolled up. He wasn't an imposing figure, but when he spoke, there was a quiet steadiness in his voice that made everyone still.

"Before you mount up," the Chaplain said, "let's take a moment. I know many of you have done this a dozen times, and some of you, this may be your first long haul. Either way, none of us walk alone."

He bowed his head. "Lord, watch over these warriors as they step into harm's way. Keep their minds sharp, their hands steady, and their hearts strong. Guide them safely to their mission and home again. Let their strength build hope, not fear, and let your grace shield them when steel and armor fall short. Amen."

A few murmured "Amen" in reply. Others just nodded and shifted their weight.

But Kevin stood there, suddenly aware of how quiet the world felt around him. He'd been on edge all day, a tension he couldn't quite name, but the prayer grounded it, gave it shape. That's when it hit him—a flicker of unease. It wasn't fear exactly. But it was concern, deep in his gut. This mission was real. And different. Something about the way the Chaplain spoke, the way everyone had listened, stuck with him.

As the team began dispersing to their vehicles, Kevin took a longer breath than usual, adjusting his gloves and checking his rifle one last time. He didn't say anything to Ray as they climbed into their truck—he didn't have to. The silence between them said plenty.

Ray took his place in the turret, settling behind the .50 cal like he was slipping into his natural element. Kevin climbed into the back seat, settling into the cramped space beside his gear, rifle across his lap.

As the engines roared to life and the gate began to open, Kevin took one last glance back toward camp. Toward the routine he was just starting to feel grounded in.

But this was the job — and this time, lives were hanging in the balance.

He adjusted his helmet, gave a nod toward Ray up in the turret, and braced for the long road ahead.

"Let's go build something that matters," he muttered to himself as the long convoy rolled forward, tires crunching over gravel, engines growling into the Afghan horizon.

Kevin's truck settled halfway in the convoy — unfortunately, right behind the fuel truck. Within minutes, the jokes started.

"Well, boys," Joe muttered from the driver's seat, adjusting his glasses, "looks like we're ridin' in the blast radius of a rolling fireball."

Ray, already standing tall in the turret behind the .50 cal, chuckled. "Perfect. We get to be roasted marshmallows if something pops off."

Kevin smirked but said nothing, glancing at the giant silver tank in front of them. The fuel truck did feel like a walking target. Every bump in the road sent a ripple through his spine and a reminder of just how far from safe they were.

Ben, the comms guy in the rear seat next to Kevin, leaned in. "They really put us behind the bomb truck, huh? I feel honored."

Dave, their fire team leader, didn't laugh. "Eyes out. Jokes don't stop RPGs."

Still, the banter helped keep the edge off. For most of the twelve-hour ride, the road passed in slow, steady hums of vibration, dust clouds, and brief radio transmissions. Occasionally, they'd see small clusters of homes — square mud structures with crumbling corners, light flickering in the distance, goats roaming aimlessly. The further they got, the more the world felt foreign and weathered by conflict.

But luck — or maybe divine mercy — stayed with them. No IEDs. No ambushes. Just miles of terrain and an endless stars overhead.

By the time the convoy approached the outskirts of Sheberghan, the sun had been up for hours, casting long, shimmering heatwaves across the horizon. A wave of relief swept through Kevin as they passed through the makeshift checkpoint into the Swiss-operated compound.

As the vehicles rolled in, the gun trucks broke off to establish a defensive perimeter around the area. Dust kicked up in thick plumes as tires dug into the dirt, forming a tight circle of protection while the engineers began planning the landing zone layout. Rolls of concertina wire were offloaded, and pallets of empty HESCO baskets were already being dragged into place with forklifts.

They weren't completely starting from scratch — Sheberghan had a small but sturdy outpost already in place. The perimeter was reinforced with 8-foot-high HESCO barriers, and there was even a proper chow hall, albeit smaller. The real blessing, though, came when they were shown to their sleeping quarters — CLUs, or Containerized Living Units only shared with one roommate. Not much bigger than shipping containers, but with AC units bolted on and bunks inside, it was practically luxury compared to tents.

The showers were another surprise — freezing cold but clean, with solid water pressure. The kind of cold that took your breath away and reminded you that you were alive, which, after twelve hours on the road behind a mobile gas can, Kevin welcomed.

He dropped his gear in his CLU, peeled off his sweat-soaked uniform, and stood in front of the AC vent for a solid two minutes before even thinking about unpacking. Outside, the whine of forklifts and voices barking orders filled the air. Work would start fast.

But for now, they'd arrived. Intact. No firefights. No explosions.

Kevin sat on the edge of his bunk and exhaled.

The next morning came early—before the sun even touched the horizon. The cool air quickly gave way to that dry, bitter heat that seemed to rise from the ground itself. Kevin scarfed down a bland breakfast in the galley and met up with the rest of the team at the trucks.

He had assumed he'd be swinging tools, maybe helping with layout or materials handling. Instead, Dave pulled him aside and handed him a pair of dusty gloves and pointed at the turret on their gun truck.

"You're on security full-time," Dave said flatly. "Second gunner. Twelve-hour shifts. You and Ray will stand watch together. Six to six."

Kevin blinked. "I've never used a fifty before."

Dave just shrugged. "You'll figure it out."

Ray grinned from under his helmet. "Think of it like an angry lawn mower that spits fire and thunder."

As Kevin climbed up into the turret and settled behind the bulky M2 .50 caliber machine gun, he was surprised by its sheer weight and size. It felt like a relic from another era—cold, mechanical, massive. He ran his hands along the charging handle, the metal already hot in the morning sun.

Dave stood beside the truck, casually pointing at the weapon. "Rack it, press the trigger, repeat until it fires."

That was the lesson. That was it.

No range time. No classroom. Just the kind of on-the-job training that came with the dirt and dust of a war zone.

Kevin spent the first hour adjusting the sights and scanning his sector of fire, feeling out the awkward stance required to stay comfortable while perched in the turret. His neck ached from craning, and his back stiffened from the posture. But over time, his movements got sharper. His eyes learned what to look for—shadows behind berms, movement in distant windows, glints off glass that didn't belong.

Down below, the rest of the crew got to work unloading material, setting forms, filling HESCOs, and compacting earth. Kevin watched from his high perch, shielding his eyes from the glare as the project slowly came together piece by piece.

Ray kept him company on and off shift, talking trash, chewing sunflower seeds, smoking almost nonstop and keeping morale up with his dry wit. Kevin quickly learned that the watch shifts were less about actual threats and more about the weight of vigilance. Twelve hours of standing still, baking in the sun, scanning a world that might or might not strike back.

"You'll go crazy if you don't learn to daydream," Ray told him during one of their shifts.

Kevin chuckled. "I'm already halfway there."

He thought about home a lot during those long hours. About his old friends, about the bar nights he used to live for, about his family who still didn't quite understand why he was here. But mostly, he thought about what it meant to be responsible now—for others, for something bigger than himself.

The .50 cal never had to fire. But Kevin stayed ready, every single day, fingers hovering near the trigger, watching that horizon like it might come alive at any moment.

And in a strange way, that constant watch brought him peace. It wasn't glamorous, but it was necessary. And for the first time in a long time, Kevin felt like he was exactly where he was supposed to be. But how did a kid from the suburbs of Chicago end up in a war tourn country of Afghanistan he would often think to himself.

Six weeks into the helicopter pad construction, the air around camp grew noticeably heavier—not from dust or heat, but from something unspoken. It started with a quiet murmur at the chow line, then traveled tent to tent like wildfire. By noon, the news had made it to every corner of the FOB.

The local Taliban had issued a demand: release their imprisoned commander from the Sheberghan prison—just two miles down the road—or face an all-out assault on the base. The threat was blunt and terrifying. Kill everyone, they'd said.

Kevin was in the turret when the word was passed down through the chain of command. Dave approached the truck, his expression grim but steady.

"Taliban's making noise," he said, his voice low. "They want their guy out of the prison. Army says no. Threats are flying."

Kevin gripped the handles of the .50 cal, scanning the horizon. "They serious?"

Dave nodded. "Could be bluff. Could be a real fight. We're prepping like it's real."

Ray climbed up beside Kevin in the turret, chew in his lip. "Shit's getting spicy, huh?"

The pit in Kevin's stomach grew heavier. He wasn't afraid to admit it—he was worried. The idea of an actual attack wasn't some abstract training scenario anymore. It was real. And it was close. But beneath the anxiety, there was a quiet resolve. Kevin was ready—ready for whatever came next, ready to fight, and if it came to it, ready to die for his team. That was the kind of bond they had. That was the kind of brotherhood they'd built.

Kevin leaned into the truck and looked at Ray. "If I'm gonna be up behind that gun looking like an easy target, the least you can do is give me a cigarette."

Ray glanced over with a smirk. "You don't smoke, Kev."

Kevin shrugged, a crooked grin on his face. "I do now."

Inside the camp, the engineers worked faster, but everyone's eyes kept drifting to the outer berms. Radios stayed hot. Perimeters were checked twice. Ammunition was double counted. Kevin spent his entire shift behind the .50 cal, gloves tightened, helmet strapped, sweat trickling down his spine.

And then came the rumble of rotors.

Two Apache attack helicopters broke across the skyline first, slicing through the air low and fast. Right behind them, two Black-hawk helicopters hovered in deliberate, circling sweeps around the perimeter of the town. It was unmistakable—a show of force.

Kevin watched the Apache's fly overhead, their rocket pods and chain guns glinting in the light, and he let out a slow breath.

"Damn," he muttered, "now that's a sight."

Ray nodded. "A little insurance policy."

The show worked. Whether it was fear, caution, or just strategic retreat, the attack never came. No mortars, no gunfire, no swarming fighters charging the gates. Just an eerie calm that settled in by dusk, the threat lingering like a shadow that never stepped into the light.

But Kevin didn't forget the feeling of those tense hours—every second behind the weapon, every glance toward the hills. It was a lesson. War wasn't always loud. Sometimes it was waiting… waiting for something to happen and praying it didn't.

That night, as he lay in his CLU staring at the ceiling, Kevin knew he'd crossed another invisible threshold. He was no longer the same man who had arrived a week ago, unsure of his weapon, unsure of his place. He wasn't scared anymore.

As the last days in Sheberghan wrapped up, Kevin found himself standing once more in the turret of his truck, watching the final pallets of gear get strapped down and the convoy forming up for the long ride back to Mazar-i-Sharif. The project was complete—the helicopter pad finished, the HESCOs filled, the perimeter reinforced. The Sweden forces had what they needed, and Kevin's team had done their job with grit and pride.

But a weight still lingered in Kevin's chest.

The twelve-hour convoy back felt different this time. It wasn't anticipation or excitement—it was reflection. The roads stretched endlessly in front of them, twisting past the same dusty villages and crumbling mud compounds they'd seen on the way in. As Kevin sat in the back passenger seat of his truck, boots propped awkwardly against the seat in front of him, he stared out the window at flickers of light in distant homes.

Small oil lamps. Dim lanterns. Occasional flashes of generator-powered bulbs.

And for a moment, he forgot where he was.

In the quiet of that cab, with the hum of the engine beneath him and the cool nighttime air filtering through the gun turret, Kevin closed his eyes and imagined he was somewhere else entirely. Maybe cruising down the interstate, a road trip back from the Wisconsin Dells. He pictured his sister asleep in the backseat, his mom up front flipping through CDs, and his dad humming along to classic rock. The idea was so vivid, so comforting, that Kevin let himself believe it—just for a few miles.

But soon enough, the real world returned.

Back at the main camp in Deh Dahdi, things fell into rhythm quickly. Kevin rejoined his old ECP team and fell back into the routine—early mornings, long inspections, and endless gravel trucks rolling in and out through the gate. The rotation felt familiar, but something inside him had shifted.

Each time a truck approached; Kevin's pulse ticked higher. He knew the drill—check under the frame, mirror the wheel wells, scan the driver's eyes for nervous ticks—but the mental wear crept in slowly. There was no glamour in the task, just a constant thread of danger masked behind routine. Every horn honk or engine backfire made him flinch. Every driver might be the one hiding something deadly beneath a tarp of gravel. But when Kevin did his personnel searches, he found a strange kind of comfort in the reactions—if the person giggled when he got close to their groin area, he knew they weren't hiding anything serious. It was an odd tell, but it worked.

At night, Kevin lay in his rack staring at the tent ceiling, unable to sleep until exhaustion finally crushed him. Sometimes he'd close his eyes and whisper to himself, "Tomorrow might be it." Not out of fear—but resolve. A quiet mantra to keep himself grounded. To stay sharp.

He was only twenty-three, and already he felt older. More weathered. More aware of how quickly things could change.

He didn't tell anyone—not Brad, not Ray, not Sean—but there were mornings he didn't want to crawl out of bed and throw on his gear. There were days where the sun felt too hot, the sand too thick, and the work too heavy for a guy just trying to do the right thing.

Still, Kevin showed up. Every shift. Every search. Every truck.

He hadn't broken—but he could feel the cracks forming at the edges.

And somewhere deep down, he knew that eventually, he'd need to face them.

As the days passed and the sun slowly began to shift lower in the sky each evening, Kevin found a new rhythm in the monotony of deployment—one that revolved less around gravel trucks and more around Jessy.

It started innocently enough. Just dinner. A familiar face in the chow line. A place saved at the table. A casual conversation that became the highlight of his day.

Every evening, Kevin would spot her just before the galley line curved around the steam trays. Jessy's hair tucked neatly into her cover, uniform always dusted from the mess hall, eyes tired but always offering him a quick grin. It didn't matter how bad his day was—seeing her made something in his chest lighten. Something hopeful.

They sat together every night now. Sometimes with Brad, Ray and Sean, who continued their relentless teasing like two middle schoolers who couldn't resist stirring the pot. Other nights it was just the two of them, tucked away at a corner table near the back wall, eating quietly and talking about things far beyond Afghanistan.

Kevin had started this quiet tradition of stealing Jessy's kiwi from her tray—every night without fail. The first time she pretended to be annoyed, swatting his hand and shaking her head. "That's the best part," she said, half laughing.

"That's why I take it," he'd replied with a smirk. "You don't appreciate it like I do."

Soon it became their inside joke. He'd snatch the fruit before she even sat down, and she'd make a mock scene of indignation.

The little moments added up. They laughed more. Talked longer. Shared stories from home, from childhood, from the dreams they hadn't yet chased.

And somewhere between those quiet dinners and sunset walks around the camp's perimeter fence, Kevin realized he was falling for her.

He hadn't planned for it. Hell, he'd convinced himself it wasn't the right time or place. But there was no denying it anymore—his heart was in it. She was more than a distraction, more than a friend. She was the calm in the chaos, the one person who made him forget, even briefly, that they were in a warzone.

Jessy talked about her plans when they got back. She wanted to take a cross-country trip, see the Las Vegas lights, maybe go back to school. Kevin listened intently, absorbing every word, storing them away like they were sacred. He didn't always share as much, but when he did, it was real—his dreams of owning a small home, fixing up old cars, maybe even starting a family one day.

They didn't say the word "relationship." They didn't need to. It was in their eyes, their tone, the way she leaned her shoulder just slightly toward him when they walked back from chow. It was in the way Kevin would sneak her an extra protein bar from his care package or how she would save him a dessert on nights he worked late.

There was only a month left in deployment, and they both felt it—the rush of time, the urgency to make every second count, and the unspoken hope that whatever this was didn't end in the dirt and dust of Afghanistan.

And somewhere in that final stretch of desert days, Kevin found himself wondering—not if they would make it work back home… but how he could make sure they did.

The final day had come. The long-anticipated moment that once felt like a far-off dream now sat heavy in the air, buzzing with energy and emotion. Gear was packed tight into sea bags and pelican cases, pallets were loaded, and boots stomped across gravel for the last time in Mazar-i-Sharif. Kevin stood quietly near the transport trucks, his helmet clipped to his pack, scanning the camp that had shaped so much of him. He didn't say much, just took it all in—the ECP, the tents, the guard towers silhouetted in the morning haze. After 6 months it was time to go.

The first leg of the journey took them back to Kuwait—the same dusty camp where Kevin had once sat for a week, anxious and unsure of what Afghanistan would hold. Now, that same place served as a decompression zone. A transition space between two worlds—combat and home.

The pace slowed in Kuwait. The urgency of missions was replaced with movies under large canopies, late-night card games, and endless conversations in the rec tents. Kevin spent those days with Ray, Sean, Brad, and Jessy—his crew, his brothers, and her.

They played cornhole tournaments, challenged each other on ping-pong tables, and watched cheesy horror movies that they narrated over with sarcastic commentary. The bond they'd built in Afghanistan only strengthened with every laugh; every story retold for the tenth time. Even the jokes felt lighter now—less like a release valve, more like celebration.

Mandatory briefs filled part of the days—PowerPoints from senior leadership reminding them of the challenges ahead. "Don't drink too much your first weekend back." "Avoid getting into fights." "Give your family time to adjust to you again—and vice versa." The instructors said it all with the tired tone of people who'd seen too many young sailors come home reckless.

Kevin listened, nodding, but his mind often wandered. He thought about his parents—how they'd reacted when he first joined and how much they'd changed over the year. He thought about his ECP team, about the gravel trucks and the countless drivers he inspected, wondering if he'd ever forget their faces. He thought about the convoys, the gun truck, that 50-cal he'd manned for hours on end. He thought about the fear he'd felt when the Taliban threatened their FOB in Sheberghan, and the overwhelming relief when those helicopters appeared overhead.

And then, of course, there was Jessy.

She sat next to him on the flight. He hadn't asked for it, but somehow it just worked out that way—like most things between them. When they boarded the massive military aircraft, she took the seat beside him and gave him a soft smile as she buckled in. Kevin leaned his head back against his seat, the vibrations of the engines starting to hum beneath them. He closed his eyes for a moment.

The six months of deployment replayed in his mind like a highlight reel—ECP shifts, convoy routes, the dust storms, the camaraderie, the jokes in the tent, stolen kiwi's, shared glances with Jessy. He felt a wave of gratitude swell in his chest.

He didn't come out of Afghanistan untouched—no one ever really did—but he came out whole. And maybe, just maybe, better than when he went in.

Jessy nudged his arm gently, pulling him out of his thoughts.

"Hey," she whispered over the engine noise, "You, okay?"

Kevin looked at her and nodded. "Yeah," he said, offering a quiet grin. "Just thinking how crazy all this has been."

She nodded too. "Crazy. But… worth it?"

Kevin turned to look back down the aisle at his teammates—Brad telling some loud story to Sean, Ray nodding off with his arms crossed. Then back to Jessy.

"Yeah," he said, "Definitely worth it."

The plane lifted off into the sky, heading west—toward California, toward home, toward whatever came next.

Part Three: Post Deployment

It didn't take long for the crew to start slipping back into their old selves after returning stateside. That first week home was a whirlwind of paperwork, uniform returns, and check-ins, but once the dust settled, it was time to celebrate. Dave, Kevin's once fire team leader, now living in a rental house with Joe and Ben, took the initiative to host the first proper party. The kind of party they'd talked about in the tent under a humming fan or in the gun trucks while watching the horizon blur into desert.

The house was already bumping by the time Kevin pulled up. Music poured out from the backyard, laughter echoing over the fence. A keg sat in the grass surrounded by red plastic cups, and smoke from the grill drifted into the twilight air. It was exactly the kind of chaos they'd all fantasized about while sweating in body armor.

Ray greeted Kevin with a loud "You finally made it, you bastard!" and handed him a drink before he even got past the porch. Brad was already halfway through his third beer, bragging about how many girls had checked him out at the grocery store that morning. Sean, as usual, was retelling one of his ridiculous jokes, already wheezing in laughter before he reached the punchline.

Jessy arrived not long after, dressed casually in jeans and a hoodie, her hair down and a soft smile on her face. Kevin's heart jumped a little when he saw her. This felt different now—stateside, real life.

But as the night wore on and the beer kept flowing, Kevin could feel himself slipping into old habits. He laughed louder, drank faster, and by the time the music turned up and a few people started dancing in the kitchen, he realized Jessy was nowhere in sight.

He found her out front, standing near her car.

"You leaving already?" he asked, slurring slightly.

Jessy gave him a kind smile, but it didn't mask her disappointment. "Yeah… this just really isn't my scene. I'm not much for parties. Never really have been."

Kevin rubbed the back of his neck. "I get that. But I was hoping we'd get to hang out more."

Jessy nodded. "I was too. But I'm not trying to compete with a party or a six-pack for your attention."

Kevin frowned, a little taken aback.

Jessy stepped closer. "Kevin… if you really like me—if you actually want to be with me—then come find me tomorrow. When you're sober."

She got in her car and drove off, leaving Kevin standing there on the sidewalk, the sounds of the party muffled behind him.

That night, he drank a few more beers, tried to laugh at more jokes, but it didn't feel the same anymore. The buzz wasn't as warm. The conversations weren't as deep. Something was missing.

The next morning, his head pounding and his breath tasting like regret, Kevin made his way to Jessy's barracks room. This time, no party, no crowd, no fog in his mind—just him, clear-headed and honest.

She opened the door, and for a moment just looked at him. No words yet. Kevin took a breath.

"I'm here," he said simply.

Jessy smiled—small, but genuine—and stepped aside to let him in.

Kevin was granted post-deployment leave, and he figured he'd head home to see his family and friends—now a full year since he'd left for the Navy. It felt like a lifetime ago. The kid who had waved goodbye wasn't the same man walking back through that front door. He carried more weight now—not just in muscle, but in memory. The war had changed him in ways he hadn't fully realized yet, but home still called to him. He needed to see familiar faces, eat home-cooked meals, and try—just for a little while—to feel normal again.

The terminal at LAX buzzed with its usual chaos—blaring announcements, the shuffle of luggage wheels, and travelers hunched over charging stations. Kevin sat quietly near Gate 47, watching the boarding area slowly fill up with red-eye passengers. He had barely slept since the party at Dave's the night before and his body still hummed with the remnants of alcohol and fatigue. The idea of being crammed into a seat for the four-hour flight to Chicago wasn't appealing, but he was ready to be home—even if just for a short while.

As he leaned back in his seat, arms crossed, his eyes drifted toward the gate entrance—then he saw him.

His father.

Captain Jim Murphy, in his crisp pilot's uniform, walked purposefully toward the boarding gate with his crew. Kevin blinked in disbelief and sat up straight. Of course, it made sense—his dad still flew for a major airline, and it was always a possibility their paths would cross in the skies. But this? This was something else entirely.

Jim spotted Kevin and gave a small, proud smile. "I made some phone calls, and it looks like I'll be flying you home tonight."

Kevin chuckled. "Guess I'm in good hands then."

Boarding the flight felt surreal. Kevin found his seat in the middle of the plane, watching as his dad passed by on his way to the cockpit. The flight attendants, likely briefed on the situation, treated Kevin with quiet reverence. One offered him a beer during the drink service, then another—maybe thinking he hadn't heard the first time. He politely declined both times. Not because he didn't want one, but because his head still throbbed from the heavy drinking the night before.

Somewhere over Nebraska, while the cabin lights were dimmed and passengers dozed off beneath thin airline blankets, Kevin leaned his head back against the seat and thought about how strange it all felt. He was flying home, literally under his father's guidance—something poetic about that. And yet, he felt detached. Uneasy.

After landing at O'Hare in the early morning hours, Kevin and Jim met up with Kevin's mother Lisa, at a cozy cafe not far from their suburban home. The sky outside was still dark, but the smell of pancakes and coffee warmed the quiet booth they sat in. His parents beamed across the table, clearly relieved to have him home—even if just for a week.

Lisa held his hand for a moment across the table. "You look healthy, Kev. Tired, but healthy."

He smiled faintly. "Yeah. It's good to be home."

But beneath the surface, Kevin already felt himself slipping back into old rhythms. The house smelled the same, the couch felt the same, and his old friends were only a phone call away. The same cycle returned almost immediately—wake up late, crack a beer while watching the Cubs, drift through the day, drink again by evening. It was as if the six months of structure and clarity had melted into the carpeting of his parents' basement.

One afternoon, Kevin and his friend Danny sat downstairs with a couple beers, the TV flickering a baseball game in the background.

They talked about old times, laughed about high school stories, and for a while, it all felt normal.

Then the storm rolled in.

A low rumble shook the windows and fat drops of rain began smacking the house. Danny barely noticed, but Kevin had tensed slightly. Then—a flash of lightning, followed instantly by a violent crack of thunder that sounded like it struck just outside the house.

Kevin jumped out of his seat, heart racing, breath caught in his throat. Before he even realized what he was doing, he had sprinted up the basement stairs. He stood frozen in the kitchen doorway, chest heaving, staring at his mother who had just been pouring herself a glass of water.

She turned toward him, startled. "Kev? You okay?"

He blinked rapidly, looking around as if confused by where he was. "Yeah… yeah, I'm fine."

But he wasn't. That was the first sign. A momentary lapse. A reaction that didn't make sense in his old world but made perfect sense in the one he'd just come from. The war hadn't followed him home—not in the way most people imagined—but something inside him had shifted, and it was starting to show.

Kevin tossed his duffle bag into the back of Danny's new pickup truck, the early morning sun just beginning to break over the suburban rooftops. It was time to head west—to California, back to the base, back to the life he wasn't sure he wanted anymore. But this time, he wasn't making the trip alone. Danny was in the driver's seat, sunglasses already on, a playlist ready to roll. The open road stretched ahead, and it felt good to be going somewhere again.

Their first stop was in Des Moines, Iowa—a good stopping point on the long trek west and the new home of Mike, their old childhood friend. Mike had settled in Iowa quickly after welding school, picking up work and finding a decent little house just outside downtown. It was good to see him again, to catch up after many years. Jessy had traveled separately, meeting them in Des Moines. She'd recently returned home to St. Joseph, Missouri, and didn't want to make the long drive back to California alone—plus, she needed to bring her car. With her backpack slung over her shoulder and a warm smile on her face, she was ready for the road ahead. She hugged Kevin tightly, the familiar scent of her shampoo triggering something comforting and grounding in him.

With the crew together—Kevin, Jessy, Danny, and Mike—the next leg of the trip kicked off. Spirits were high as Danny and Mike climbed into the truck, while Jessy and Kevin took her car, now packed to the brim with gear, snacks, and all the road trip essentials.

The miles rolled by under the tires as the sun dipped low across the horizon, painting the sky in warm streaks of orange and pink. Kevin kept one hand on the wheel, the other draped casually over the console, while Jessy sat cross-legged in the passenger seat, sipping from a bottle of water. The music played softly in the background, but most of the time, it was their conversation that filled the space. They talked about everything—childhood stories, embarrassing high school moments, favorite movies, weird food habits. Kevin laughed when Jessy admitted she still slept with a fan on year-round, even in winter. Jessy raised an eyebrow when Kevin revealed he'd never seen *The Notebook*.

"How have you made it this far in life without watching at least one cheesy love movie?" she teased, bumping his arm. He grinned,

"Guess I was waiting for someone to force me." The hours melted away, and with each mile, they weren't just traveling across states—they were building something, quietly and effortlessly, one conversation at a time.

Their route would take them through Colorado's winding mountain highways, across high plains, and finally into the electric neon chaos of Las Vegas before reaching their final destination in Port Hueneme.

Colorado offered beautiful scenery and a much-needed break from long stretches of interstate. The group stopped at a small roadside diner nestled in a pine-lined valley, laughing over greasy burgers and recounting old deployment stories. The night they spent in a cabin just outside Denver was full of card games, beers around a campfire, and jokes that only people who'd grew up together could truly understand.

But it was in Las Vegas where things started to shift.

The city welcomed them in its typical loud, intoxicating way—flashing lights, crowded casinos, blaring music, and endless temptations. The group booked a suite for three nights at a mid-tier hotel on the strip; a little over their budget but worth the splurge for the experience. Kevin, caught up in the energy of it all, began drinking more heavily than usual. The beers became whiskey, the shots doubled, and the laughs louder. Jessy wasn't impressed. She didn't say anything at first, but the concern was in her eyes.

Still, even in the glitz and haze of Vegas, something real happened. On their second night in the city, Kevin surprised Jessy with tickets to the Beatles LOVE Cirque Du Soleil show. He hadn't said anything about it—just told her to dress nice and meet him in the hotel lobby. When she arrived, her eyes widened with surprise and delight.   The bright lights of the Las Vegas Strip shimmered in the night as Kevin and Jessy walked towards The Mirage from the strip.

The grand facade of the casino gleamed with golden accents and towering palm trees swayed in the warm desert breeze. Inside, the air buzzed with energy—clinking slot machines, the low hum of conversation, and the scent of perfume mixed with a hint of cigars and polished marble. They made their way through the dazzling casino floor, past cascading waterfalls and lush indoor gardens, until they reached the entrance to the Beatles LOVE Theater.

The atmosphere shifted the moment they stepped in—psychedelic murals, vintage Beatles memorabilia, and iconic lyrics painted along the walls set the tone. A soft glow bathed the theater in color as the crowd filtered in, buzzing with anticipation. Kevin looked around, impressed.

"This place is wild," he said, taking Jessy's hand. She smiled,

"Just wait—it's not even started yet." They found their seats and settled in, the lights dimming just as a wave of music rolled over the audience—the opening notes of a Beatles classic. The curtain rose, and the next hour was a kaleidoscope of sound, light, and movement—dancers twirling midair, acrobats soaring across the stage, and a symphony of color weaving through iconic songs. Kevin sat wide-eyed, lost in the surreal magic of it all, while Jessy leaned close and whispered, "Told you it'd be unforgettable."

"This is our first real date," Kevin said sheepishly "I figured it should be something different."

It was more than different—it was perfect. The music, the acrobatics, the colors—it was magic. Jessy leaned her head on Kevin's shoulder halfway through the show, and when the curtain finally dropped, they didn't rush to leave. Instead, they sat in silence for a moment, letting the experience sink in.

Later that night, back in their suite, Kevin kissed her. There wasn't some grand confession or dramatic moment—just the quiet understanding that something had changed between them. They were no longer just friends. Something deeper had started.

And so, in the middle of the most chaotic city on earth, Kevin and Jessy became official—two people trying to figure out what came next in a world they were still trying to readjust to.

Returning to Port Hueneme felt like a different kind of deployment for Kevin—one without enemy threats but filled with its own battles. After a short post-deployment leave, he was assigned to a new platoon: CSE—Convoy Security Element. It was a respected assignment, built for Seabees who could handle the intensity and responsibility of guarding the convoys that kept everything moving downrange. To Kevin's satisfaction, both Brad and Ray were assigned to his truck again. Their bond remained strong, a continuation of what they'd forged overseas. The laughter, the banter, the quiet understanding of what they'd endured—it all carried over.

Sean, however, had moved on. His enlistment had ended, and he returned home to Michigan with his wife, trading war stories for bedtime stories. Today, Sean works as a sales agent for automated machinery and is a proud father of two. Kevin still calls him from time to time, often reminiscing about the old days or checking in on life back home. Their friendship endured, even as their paths grew further apart.

CSE training was nothing like Kevin had experienced before. It was rigorous, built to simulate real-world threats and combat scenarios. The days were long and packed with convoy drills, close quarters combat (CQC) training, and crew-served weapons handling. Kevin got used to the thump of 240 Bravo machine guns, the clatter of gear, and the intensity of full-kit live fire exercises. The two-month training cycle was capped with a grueling week in the field, where every meal came from an MRE and sleep was a luxury.

The stress and demands of training drove many in the platoon to adopt the unofficial mantra: "Work hard, play harder." The weekends turned into an outlet—bars, house parties, drinking until memories blurred. Kevin fell back into the rhythm easily, almost too easily. The drinking became heavier, more frequent. It wasn't just celebration anymore—it was routine.

It didn't escape Jessy's attention.

As she and Kevin became more serious, her concerns grew louder. Jessy's mother's struggles with alcohol had left deep scars, ones she had tried to escape by joining the Navy in the first place. But instead of escaping it, she found herself right back in its orbit—this time through Kevin.

She spoke up one night after a particularly wild weekend. "I joined the Navy to get away from this," she said quietly as they sat on the edge of his bed. "I don't want to go through what I watched my mom go through. And I don't want to be with someone who's going to walk that same path."

Kevin didn't take it seriously at first. He thought she was just being overly cautious, thought she'd eventually loosen up and join the partying. But she never did. Jessy stood firm, uncomfortable in the haze of alcohol-fueled nights that were now Kevin's norm.

The tension grew. Jessy eventually told Kevin she was thinking of breaking up. She couldn't see a future if he continued down this path. That hit Kevin hard. He promised her he'd cut back—that he'd find balance and be better. For a little while, he did. He skipped a few parties, drank a little less, tried to show her he was serious.

But it didn't last.

The momentum of CSE life, the camaraderie, the stress, the culture—it kept pulling him back in. He wanted to be better for her but deep down, he wasn't ready to let go of that lifestyle.

Kevin was fighting a quiet battle no one else could see. Most nights, he'd jolt awake in a panic—heart pounding, drenched in sweat, eyes wide as if he were still behind the .50 cal in Sheberghan or searching a gravel truck at the ECP. His body tensed before his mind could catch up. It took him a few seconds to realize he was in his barracks room, safe, far from any threat. The cycle became routine—wake up in terror, breathe, try to shake it off, go back to sleep. He never mentioned it to anyone, not even Jessy.

"It's not PTSD," he told himself again and again. "I was never in a firefight… never even shot at." But deep down, he knew something wasn't right. He just didn't have the words for it yet, and maybe he didn't want to.

When the next deployment orders came in, Kevin found himself on a humanitarian detachment to Cambodia. It was a different kind of mission—no convoys, no body armor, no threat of incoming fire. His detachment was tasked with drilling water wells and supporting local villages with infrastructure projects. The change of pace was welcomed.

Jessy, meanwhile, had been sent to Okinawa with the main body of NMCB 40. Although separated by oceans and different missions, they kept in touch every single night. Their conversations were a comfort—something stable and familiar in a world that constantly shifted.

In Cambodia, Kevin poured his energy into something new. He studied hard for his Seabee Combat Warfare Device, putting in hours of memorization and hands-on practice until he earned the pin proudly worn on his uniform. Around the same time, he picked up his next rank—UT3. Both milestones felt like real achievements, not just checkboxes on a Navy career sheet.

He also began to focus on his physical and mental health. He hit the gym five days a week, getting into the best shape of his life. The weight room became his release, a place to sweat out his demons rather than drown them in whiskey. He still went out with the guys sometimes—had a beer here and there—but the wild partying was a thing of the past. He found peace in his routine, in his progress, in his discipline.

For the first time in a long time, Kevin felt like he was on the right path—not just as a sailor, but as a man. And for the first time, he realized he didn't need to be numb to feel okay. He just needed purpose.

After nine months overseas, Kevin stepped off the bus in Port Hueneme, California, greeted by the familiar ocean breeze and the crisp sound of boots on asphalt. His second deployment had come to a close, and with it came a sense of accomplishment—and exhaustion. A few days later, Jessy returned as well, and the two reunited with a quiet embrace that said everything words couldn't.

But things were changing fast. The Navy, amidst downsizing, had made the decision to decommission NMCB 40. The battalion that had shaped so much of Kevin and Jessy's early careers was being dissolved. Sailors were given options: if they had completed at least two years of their enlistment, they could voluntarily separate from the service. For many, it was an unexpected exit ramp. For others, like Kevin, it was just another fork in the road.

Jessy, however, had made up her mind. She'd done her time, seen the world, and now wanted something different. Civilian life had been calling her for some time, and the decommissioning of NMCB 40 felt like a clean, natural endpoint. Kevin understood, even respected it—though deep down, he wasn't ready to hang up his uniform just yet.

After long talks over late-night dinners and quiet weekends together, they came to a decision: Jessy would separate from the Navy, and they would move in together. They both knew it would be a transition, but it was one they were ready to take on as a team. It felt like the right step forward—growing together in a new phase of life.

The day NMCB 40 officially decommissioned, Jessy received her DD214. Kevin stood by her side, proud, as she turned the page on her chapter of service. He, meanwhile, transitioned over to NMCB 3, ready to continue his journey for the remaining two years of his contract.

While their paths were beginning to look different, their foundation felt solid. For the first time in a long time, Kevin felt like life was beginning to take shape beyond the uniform—even if he wasn't done wearing it just yet.

Another homeport rotation rolled around, and this time, Kevin stepped back into CSE with a new sense of confidence and purpose. He wasn't just another guy in the truck anymore—he was experienced now, seasoned by convoys through warzones, long nights under the stars behind a .50 cal, and lessons learned the hard way. He knew the ins and outs of convoy operations, the small details that kept teams safe and the bigger lessons that kept them sane. This time, Kevin wasn't just a participant—he was a mentor.

The new faces in the platoon looked to him for guidance, and Kevin took that role seriously. He taught by example, steady under pressure and calm in chaos, passing on small bits of wisdom like how to read a driver's body language at a checkpoint, or the best way to troubleshoot a comms failure mid-mission. He knew what it meant to shoulder responsibility—not just for himself, but for the guy next to him.

Brad had since moved on, transferring to the East Coast for a new challenge. He was now working with Naval Special Warfare Group 2 (NSWG2), attached to LOGSU—supporting logistics missions with SEAL Teams 2 and 10. True to his nature, Brad bragged constantly in their group chats about his new assignment, but everyone knew he'd earned it. Kevin was proud of him. They'd started as rowdy young Seabees cracking jokes in tents, and now they were evolving, finding their places in the wider fleet.

As Kevin continued to train hard with CSE, he started to see his career from a wider lens—not just as a Seabee, but as a leader. He still had his struggles, sure. He still fought the lingering anxiety that crept in during quiet nights. But he also felt a renewed sense of purpose in helping shape the next wave of Seabees.

While Kevin settled into his new role with CSE in NMCB 3, he was glad to find that Ray had also made the move over—but was now assigned to Bravo Company. Though they weren't working side by side like they had in Afghanistan, and again in the same truck for CSE the year prior, their bond didn't fade. The camaraderie built in tents and gun trucks wasn't easily replaced.

Even with different schedules and responsibilities, Kevin and Ray made it a point to stay close. Weekends became their time to reconnect—barbecues at Kevin's place, late-night bonfires on the beach, or just sitting on the porch talking about everything and nothing. It was a comfort to have someone around who truly understood where they'd come from and what they'd been through.

Sometimes they talked about the old days, laughing about Sean's jokes or Brad's endless bragging. Other times, the conversations got deeper—about the toll deployments took, about the weird panic that still crept into quiet moments, and how strange civilian life looked from their side of the fence. There was an unspoken agreement between the two: no judgment, just understanding.

Even as Kevin matured into his leadership role, Ray remained one of the few people who could get him to let his guard down and just be Kevin—not UT3, not a CSE mentor, just the guy from the tent in Mazar-i-Sharif who still carried those moments with him every day.

Kevin had been planning the day for weeks—a trip to Universal Studios with Jessy and Ray, under the disguise of just a fun outing before the next training cycle kicked into full swing. But in Kevin's pocket, nestled deep in the fabric of his jacket, was the real reason for the trip: a small velvet box that held a ring and a big question.

It had become an inside joke between him and Jessy to point at random places on hikes or drives and claim, "That's where they filmed Jurassic Park." It always got a laugh, especially because Jessy would call him out immediately. The Jurassic Park ride was the backdrop Kevin had chosen, and the plan was simple   pose for a photo, then drop to one knee while Ray captured the moment forever.

But the day before their trip, Kevin made a call that weighed heavy on him. He dialed Jessy's dad, Monty—a man he'd only met once, briefly, due to the distance between California and Monty's home in Kansas. Kevin wanted to do it right. He wanted to show respect. But when he asked for Monty's blessing, the answer hit hard.

"No," Monty said. "I don't give my blessing. You're not a man of God."

The words stung more than Kevin expected, but he stayed composed. He didn't argue. He just said thank you and hung up. Disappointed, sure—but not deterred. He wasn't asking to marry Monty. He was asking Jessy. The woman who stood by him through deployments, through his drinking, through the growing pains of becoming a better man. And he'd already decided—he was going to do this.

The next day, at the park, Kevin tried to act normal, but his nerves danced behind every laugh and smile. They rode rides, ate junk food, and snapped photos. When they finally made it to the Jurassic Park ride, Kevin gave Ray a subtle nod. Jessy stood between them, laughing and ready to pose for another picture. But as she turned toward the camera, Kevin dropped to one knee and opened the box.

Her face froze, eyes wide, hands going to her mouth in shock. Ray caught it all—the exact moment Jessy realized what was happening. Kevin didn't say much. He didn't need to. His expression said it all. Jessy smiled through tears and nodded before even saying the words.

"Yes."

With the ring on Jessy's finger and excitement still fresh, the wedding planning quickly took shape. Jessy dove into ideas for venues, dresses, and guest lists, while Kevin balanced his role as a supportive fiancé with preparing for his third deployment—this time to the remote islands of Tonga for another humanitarian mission. It was only a six-month rotation, but it still meant another stretch apart.

Before he left, they promised to keep their routine strong—just like before. Daily calls, texts when possible, and always finding a way to keep each other close, even across the miles. Kevin had grown used to the rhythm of separation and reunion, but this time, with wedding plans in the background, it felt different—more urgent, more meaningful.

In Tonga, Kevin pushed hard like he always did. The mission was rewarding—clean water systems, infrastructure repairs, and real, visible impact. The deployment flew by. He wasn't the wide-eyed new guy anymore. He was seasoned, confident, and focused. His effort didn't go unnoticed—he was promoted to UT2 during that deployment. The announcement came on a humid afternoon, and though Kevin celebrated with his team, the first thing he did was call Jessy.

"You're marrying a second class petty officer now," he joked.

She laughed. "Good. Then you can afford nicer centerpieces."

But with that promotion came a decision—re-enlist or separate. Kevin stood at a crossroads. Ray had picked up UT2 the year before and was planning to stay in, considering shore duty or a shot at becoming an instructor. Kevin wasn't so sure. He loved the Seabees, the work, the camaraderie—but something was pulling him in a different direction.

One option stood out: recruiting duty. It would be a new challenge, a break from deployments, and a chance to grow in a different way. He brought the idea to Jessy.

"Let's try it," she said without hesitation. "We've done the hard part already. It's time for something new."

So, with new orders in hand, a fresh chevron on his sleeve, and a wedding just around the corner, Kevin was finally in a place of balance. He didn't have all the answers yet, but he had direction—and that was more than enough.

The wedding came fast. Friends from every chapter of Kevin's life showed up—buddies from his childhood days in the Midwest, Navy teammates from deployments and training, his family, and of course Jessy's family and closest friends. It was a rare gathering of old and new, a celebration that brought together all the people who had helped shape who they were.

Kevin and Jessy chose to get married on the Fourth of July, 2014, aboard a ferry boat venue in the Oxnard Harbor. The warm coastal breeze carried laughter and music across the water. As the sun dipped behind the Pacific, fireworks lit up the sky—red, white, and blue explosions reflecting off the harbor, turning the moment into something surreal. It was a perfect night. Romantic, loud, joyful, and unforgettable. The kind of beginning that felt straight out of a movie.

But the night before wasn't quite as magical.

Kevin had gone out with the guys for one last wild ride—Brad, Danny, Mike, Ray, even a few others from his deployments. It was chaos in the best way. Bars, shots, loud stories, and old inside jokes flowing like the booze. They partied until last call, stumbling home with hoarse voices and sore ribs from laughing too hard.

Kevin woke up the next morning in a haze—dry-mouthed, pounding head, and a stomach that turned with every movement. It was, without question, the worst hangover of his life. He laid in bed groaning, the thought of putting on a tux almost laughable.

Brad and Danny came to his rescue like seasoned pros—milkshakes, greasy breakfast sandwiches, ibuprofen, sunglasses, and unfiltered teasing. But nothing really took the edge off until Kevin cracked open a cold beer, and like flipping a switch, the fog began to lift.

That moment should've felt like a small win. But deep down, it was a subtle warning—one he didn't yet want to face.

Still, by the time he saw Jessy in her wedding dress, all that faded away. She looked radiant, standing on the deck under strings of lights, smiling like she already knew everything would be okay. As they exchanged vows surrounded by fireworks, Kevin felt lucky. Whatever came next, they were in it together.

After the wedding and a short honeymoon, Kevin and Jessy packed their things and began the next chapter of their lives together. They moved to Belvidere, Illinois, a small town just outside of Rockford, where Kevin was assigned to a Navy recruiting office. It was a far cry from the California coastline and the fast-paced rhythm of deployment life, but it was the next step—a fresh start, and one they were ready for.

Before the big move, Kevin and Jessy hosted a going-away party at their favorite spot—BJ's, a cozy pizza joint known for its deep-dish pies and ice-cold beer. It had become one of their go-to places over the years, so it felt right to say goodbye there. The place was packed with familiar faces—Ray, Joe, Dave, even a few guys from other detachments who drove in just to be there. Kevin's dad, Jim, was there too, helping with the move and soaking in the energy of the night.

Laughter echoed across the restaurant as pitchers of beer were passed around, pizzas devoured, and stories shared. One by one, the guys stood up to tell tales—half hilarious, half unbelievable—about training mishaps, drunken nights overseas, convoy close calls, and all the moments that had forged their brotherhood. Jessy smiled as she listened, realizing just how much these bonds meant to Kevin and her.

But as the night wore on and the goodbyes started, a heaviness settled in Kevin's chest. Handshakes turned into hugs, and the weight of what he was leaving behind hit him hard. These men weren't just friends—they were brothers. They'd lived, worked, fought, and grown together. And now, in one swift move, it all felt like it was being left behind.

As he walked out into the parking lot, Kevin broke down. He leaned against his truck, eyes full of tears he hadn't seen coming. The laughter and noise from the restaurant faded behind him, replaced by the ache of separation.

Jim walked up, concerned but unsure what to say. "You just had too much to drink, son," he said, trying to brush it off.

But Kevin shook his head. "It's not the beer, Dad. You just… you don't get it."

And he didn't. Not really. Jim had never worn a uniform, never felt the gravity of a goodbye like this. He couldn't understand the invisible thread that tied those men together. Kevin was stepping into a new life—but in that moment, it felt like he was leaving a part of himself behind.

Jessy came to his side, quietly wrapping her arm around his. "You're not losing them," she said softly. "You're just starting something new. The good ones—they'll always be there."

Kevin nodded, wiping his face. It didn't make it easier, but she was right.

He climbed into the truck and looked back one more time at the glowing sign of BJ's. The laughter still spilled out the doors, but he knew the chapter had closed.

Tomorrow would be the beginning of something different. But tonight—it was okay to feel the loss.

The move to Illinois came quickly. Kevin, Jessy, and Jim packed up the little rental house in California—box by box, one memory at a time. When they pulled into Belvidere, their new house immediately felt like a fresh beginning. A solid all-brick home with three bedrooms, two baths, and a two-car garage that would come in handy for snowy Midwest winters. Two tall oak trees shaded the front yard like quiet sentries, and Kevin thought, *Yeah… this could work.*

The house had character, a certain warmth to it. The basement would become Kevin's man cave—a bar tucked into the corner with bar stools, sports memorabilia, and a wall separating his tools and shop area. It was the kind of place he could disappear into after a long day, crack open a beer, and feel like he still had some control over something.

Recruiting duty started out with energy and enthusiasm. Kevin figured if he could talk about the Navy like he talked with his brothers, he'd be just fine. And for a while, it worked. He told stories—real ones—about Afghanistan, convoys, the ECP, and how the Navy had shaped him. High schoolers and walk-ins sat wide-eyed, listening. Some were eager to sign, others just enjoyed the stories. Either way, Kevin had a gift.

His new team was tight, but different. Brent was the LPO—sharp, all business, a career Aviation Ordnanceman from the fleet. Chris was a Damage Controlman who'd served most of his time on destroyers, and Amanda, a yeoman, had spent years working in admin roles out of Norfolk. They all had a certain fleet Navy swagger about them, shared jokes about ship life and port calls. But Kevin... he was the odd one out, the Seabee, the dirt Navy guy. His world had been combat boots and convoys—not flight decks and ship routines. Kevin had expeditionary skills and experience in a military branch focused on the fleet.

At first, the differences were just surface-level. But as time passed, Kevin started to feel the gap widening. He didn't quite fit in. His passion for the Navy was fading under the weight of cold calls, high school visits, and endless Facebook posts begging for attention. He was good at it—one of the top recruiters in the district even—but each day it felt like he was selling a version of the Navy he didn't fully understand anymore.

And deeper than that was the ache he couldn't shake—he missed his team. He missed the mission. He missed *belonging* to something that felt real. Ray had moved to Virginia Beach and moved in with Brad. The two of them living together again, working alongside Navy Special Warfare teams, chasing the high of purpose that Kevin now only talked about from behind a recruiter's desk.

He'd scroll through his phone at night, seeing pictures of them fishing off the coast, lifting in a gritty gym, joking around like nothing had changed. But for Kevin, everything had.

Even Jessy noticed the shift in him. He smiled less. Talked less. The fire that had carried him through three deployments and a thousand challenges now flickered quietly behind tired eyes.

He had a house, a wife who loved him, and a solid job—but still, something inside him was missing.

And he couldn't help but wonder if maybe that something had been left behind in the dust of a convoy road in Afghanistan.

Kevin never meant for it to get out of hand—it just started small. A beer or two after work to unwind, then a couple more to help him sleep. Before long, the six-pack of Coors Light became a nightly ritual, each one cracked open with a sense of resignation, not celebration. On bad days—the kind where recruiting numbers were low, or when a memory from deployment crept in too deep—it was whiskey. Shot after shot, poured in silence under the warm glow of his man cave bar lights.

It wasn't partying anymore. It was coping.

He told himself it was normal—he'd earned it. After all, he had a full bar in the basement, might as well use it. No sense in letting it go to waste. Besides, it wasn't hurting anyone… or so he thought.

But Jessy observed.

She watched the man she loved slowly slip into a fog of alcohol and self-isolation. At first, she tried to understand—telling herself it was just a phase, just stress, just adjustment. But months passed, and it only got worse.

She'd hear the clink of bottles every night, sometimes long after she'd gone to bed. The smell of booze started to follow Kevin around. His mood changed too—shorter fuse, blank stares, less laughter. Their dinner conversations turned to silence, then silence turned to arguments. The fights started every few days—then every day.

"You're not the same anymore," Jessy said one night, her voice shaking as Kevin poured another drink in front of her.

"I'm fine," he mumbled. "I'm just trying to unwind."

"It's not unwinding anymore, Kevin—it's escaping. You're not here. You're somewhere else every time you drink, and I'm tired of watching you disappear."

Kevin didn't know how to respond. Part of him wanted to scream, another part just wanted to drink until the conversation faded again.

Jessy stood her ground. She wasn't the kind to give ultimatums lightly, but she couldn't take it anymore.

"I love you, Kevin. But I'm not going to stick around and watch you drown yourself in a bottle. You need help. If you don't fix this… I'll leave."

Kevin stared at her, stunned. Not angry—just hollow. It was the first time he realized the damage wasn't just inside of him anymore—it was spreading.

He had a choice to make. And for the first time in a long time, the bottle didn't feel like the answer.

Kevin wanted to prove he could change—not just for Jessy, but for himself. So he took her words to heart and walked into an AA meeting one evening, shoulders heavy but head high. He wanted to believe this could work, that it could help him reset, get things back on track.

The room smelled like old coffee and cigarette smoke, filled with folding chairs and people clutching Styrofoam cups. Kevin sat quietly, listening as people took turns sharing their stories.

One woman's voice cracked as she recounted the day her kids walked to a bar down the street from their house to find her, begging her to come home and make them dinner. She waved them off, choosing her next drink over her children. The room nodded solemnly, but Kevin just sat there, stunned. He couldn't relate—he wasn't *that* far gone. Was he?

Then came stories that, to Kevin, sounded almost like drunken war stories—tales of blackouts, bar fights, epic benders. Some of them were dark, sure, but others were almost… entertaining. Kevin caught himself thinking *that actually sounds like a good time*, and the irony hit him like a slap in the face.

It was hard to take it seriously after that.

He tried to stay open-minded, attending a few more meetings. He even spoke once, talking vaguely about stress, the Navy, and how drinking just helped take the edge off. People listened. Some nodded. But when the conversations circled back to finding strength in God, Kevin felt himself drifting. He wasn't a man of God—and that was fine by him—but AA was built around that foundation. And without that belief, he felt like a guest in someone else's recovery.

He gave it an honest try. He really did. But he walked out of his last meeting more confused than hopeful. He wasn't in denial—he knew he had a problem. He just didn't believe AA was *his* answer.

Jessy asked him how it was going, and Kevin was honest.

"I don't know… I'm not like them. Not yet, anyway."

"That's the point, Kevin," Jessy said quietly. *"You don't want to be."*

Kevin told Jessy he'd give AA one last shot—*"What could it hurt?"* he had said.

But as he drove toward the meeting that night, something shifted in his mind. He wasn't sure why—maybe it was ego, maybe denial—but when he pulled into the parking lot, he didn't get out of the car. Instead, he looked across the street at a bar glowing in neon.

One beer. Just one, he told himself. *If I can stop at one, I'm fine. I'll prove it to myself.*

But one turned into four.

An hour passed. The meeting was over by now, so Kevin figured he might as well head home.

He never made it more than a few blocks before the red and blue lights lit up in his rearview mirror. His heart dropped.

Panic. Shame. Fear.

Not like this, he thought. *I'm supposed to be at an AA meeting, not getting pulled over drunk. If I get a DUI... I'm done. The Navy doesn't forgive that. One and done.*

His hands were shaking as he pulled over, heart pounding in his chest like a drum. *How am I going to explain this to Jessy? To Brent? To my family?*

The officer walked up. Kevin kept his eyes low, rolled down the window, and did his best to speak clearly.

"License and registration," the cop said.

Kevin handed over his license, registration, and quietly slid in his Navy ID, hoping—maybe praying—it would help.

The cop glanced at the ID and raised an eyebrow. "You're in the Navy, huh?"

"Yes, sir," Kevin replied.

The officer cracked a smile. "I was in the Army. Ten years. What's a sailor doing all the way out here in Belvidere? No ships for miles."

Kevin chuckled nervously and explained his role as a recruiter for the area.

"Well," the cop said, handing everything back, "I pulled you over for your window tints. But since you're a fellow service member, I'll let it slide tonight. Drive safe."

Kevin nodded, thanked him, and drove off slowly.

The moment the lights disappeared behind him, the weight of what *almost* happened came crashing down.

He had dodged a bullet. A DUI would've ended everything—his career, his marriage, his future. He didn't deserve that cop's kindness. He didn't deserve to walk away from that moment clean.

But he did.

And that was the last time Kevin ever took a drink.

He went home, sat in the dark basement where he'd spent so many nights drinking alone, and just stared at the bar. Everything that had seemed fun, harmless, or numbing before now looked like poison. He didn't cry, didn't scream. He just sat there in silence—knowing he had come *this close* to throwing it all away.

He hadn't hit rock bottom… but he'd looked it in the face.

And from that moment on, Kevin knew something had to change. Not for Jessy. Not for the Navy. But for himself.

A month had passed, and Kevin was doing great. No drinking. His evenings were spent with Jessy, tackling little house projects, laughing, reconnecting. Life felt lighter—hopeful even. He started to believe he could turn the page for good.

But it was more than just staying busy—Kevin had found something he was missing. He joined a local recreational hockey league, lacing up his skates a few nights a week. It wasn't combat boots and convoy missions, but it gave him a team again—camaraderie, purpose, that same push and adrenaline he'd craved since leaving his Battalion. The locker room jokes, the sweat, the noise of the rink—it filled the hole in his life he hadn't known how to fix until now.

Hockey gave Kevin something alcohol never could—a reason to feel alive without numbing himself. The discipline of showing up, the high of chasing the puck, the quiet pride of pushing his body instead of poisoning it. He didn't want to feel sluggish or sick on the ice. He didn't want to let his teammates down. The ice became his outlet, his therapy, his new bar stool—except this one came with laces, bruises, and breathless laughter instead of hangovers and regret. Each game gave him a small victory, a reminder that he was stronger than the cravings. Every time he walked into that rink, he was choosing a better version of himself. And for the first time in a long time, that choice didn't feel impossible—it felt natural. Hockey didn't just help Kevin stay sober. It helped him start healing.

One night after Kevin returned home from a hockey game, the phone lit up with Brad's name on the screen.

Kevin answered casually at first, but the second Brad spoke, he knew something was off. His voice was slow, heavy, hesitant—like it was dragging a weight behind it.

After a moment of awkward small talk, Brad dropped it.

"Ray's gone… he took his own life today."

Silence.

Kevin froze. "No… No, you're fucking with me," he said, gripping the phone tighter.

But Brad wasn't.

It was real.

Ray was gone.

The words hit like a freight train—ripping the air from Kevin's lungs. His heart sank. His mind raced. It didn't make sense. None of it made sense.

Brad, now Ray's roommate, was carrying the crushing task of calling the old ECP team one by one. His voice cracked under the weight of it all.

"No one saw it coming," he said. "He seemed fine… the same old Ray."

Kevin could barely process it. How? Why?

Ray was the guy who kept everyone laughing, who made the hard days easier, who had your back without question. But maybe behind all of that, Ray had been fighting his own war—the kind no one saw.

Kevin couldn't help but think back to those nights he'd wake up in a cold sweat, heart racing. He had Jessy there, someone to hold him, someone to pull him out of the nightmare he was just in. But Ray didn't. He had Brad. He had his parents. But maybe it wasn't enough.

Maybe no one really knew what Ray was carrying.

Kevin blamed himself—for not calling more, not visiting Virginia Beach, not being the kind of friend Ray might have needed. He should've seen the signs… but there were none. Just silence.

And now, there would always be silence.

The reality of the 2010–2011 Afghanistan deployment was something most people couldn't understand. There weren't front lines like the wars in history books—there was no battlefield marked by flags or trenches. Instead, the troops fought a ghost.

The enemy could appear at any moment. Every step outside the wire could be the last. Every convoy could end in an explosion. Every night could be the night it all went wrong.

And yet—Kevin's team was lucky. They were never shot at. They never took a casualty. They never had to fire their weapons.

But the damage was done all the same.

It was a different kind of wound—quiet, invisible. Kevin felt it almost every night. The way his heart would pound in the dark. The way his mind would replay things that never even happened but almost could have. The way he'd leap at thunder or startle awake from a dream he couldn't remember.

They came home with their bodies intact, but not everything made it back whole.

And now Ray was gone.

That truth hit harder than anything Kevin had ever faced in Afghanistan.

The war they fought didn't just stay in the desert—it followed them home. And while Kevin had managed to keep a grip, just barely, Ray had slipped through. The ghosts didn't stop chasing them when they left the wire. They just learned to hide in silence, behind smiles, in quiet rooms where no one was looking.

SEABEES

"CAN DO"

Epilogue

Brad separated from the Navy in 2018 after ten years of honorable service. He transitioned smoothly into civilian life, finding his stride working for the FAA as a generator and power grid instructor, supporting airports across the country. No longer wearing the uniform, but still serving in his own way, Brad found purpose and fulfillment in his new role—and more importantly, he was truly enjoying life.

Sean remained in Michigan, where he married his high school sweetheart. Together, they are raising two kids and building a peaceful life. Sean now works as a salesman, providing for his family and staying connected with his old Navy brothers through the occasional phone call or visit. Though far from the days of convoys and deployment, the bond between him and the others remains strong.

As of writing this book in 2025, Kevin is still proudly married to Jessy. Together, they're raising two boys—now six and eight years old—full of energy, laughter, and life. Their home is in Long Beach, Mississippi, where the ocean breeze rolls in, and the past feels just a little bit farther away.

Kevin continues to serve in the Navy, dedicated as ever, with retirement on the horizon in 2030. After everything—the deployments, the battles fought both overseas and within—he's still standing, still serving, and still holding tight to the things that matter most.

This story wasn't always easy to tell. There was pain, loss, struggle, and growth. But through it all, there was also love, friendship, purpose—and hope.

And in the end, maybe that's what matters most.

Thank You for Reading

If this story moved you, resonated with you, or offered a glimpse into a world you hadn't seen before, I'd be truly grateful if you took a moment to leave an honest review.

Your words help future readers discover this book—and they mean more than you know.

Thank you for your support.